Follow *the* Sun

"Come off it, Rachel — you must think I'm really stupid. What do you think this is then, eh?" Jack scrabbled in his pocket, pulled out the crumpled photograph of Rachel with Gerald and brandished it in front of her face.

Rachel gaped at the photo in horror. It was like being confronted by a nightmare. "Where did that come from?" she asked in a faint whisper.

"Does it really matter?" Jack asked wearily, as though his worst fears had been confirmed. "All that matters is that you are a lying, scheming two-timer who's deceived me and deceived Dream Ticket."

Also in the Point Romance series

Look out for:

Follow the Sun

Amber Vane

■SCHOLASTIC

Scholastic Children's Books
Commonwealth House, 1–19 New Oxford Street,
London WC1A 1NU, UK
a division of Scholastic Ltd
London ~ New York ~ Toronto ~ Sydney ~ Auckland

First published by Scholastic Ltd, 1996
Copyright © Amber Vane, 1996

ISBN 0 590 13708 5
Typeset by TW Typesetting, Midsomer Norton, Avon
Printed by Cox & Wyman Ltd, Reading, Berks.

The right of Amber Vane to be identified as the author
of this work has been asserted by her in accordance with the
Copyright, Designs and Patents Act, 1988.

1

Rachel loved the evenings best. All day the sun had been blazing down from a fierce blue sky, scorching the beach so that it was impossible to go barefoot along the white-hot sand. It had been too hot to walk, too hot to sit, too hot even to lie on the beach unless you plunged into the sea every two minutes.

For once, she had been pleased to have to stay indoors, looking after the Dream Ticket under-tens. At least the Seashell Club was cool and shady. And after the intense heat outside it felt comfortingly normal to be playing Snap! with a dozen rowdy children.

But now was the perfect time. The olive trees along the beach glistened in the fading light as the brilliant red sun began to dim. A few swimmers lingered in the ocean, a few lovers straggled along the shore, the shops in the square and the tavernas dotting the coast road were beginning to reopen after the long afternoon siesta. Best of all, work was over for the day. There was time for a swim in the pool, a quick shower, and then everyone was going to meet up for a barbecue at Andy's, right on the beach. As it was a special evening, Andy had promised them some surprises.

"I hope it's nothing too exotic," Lisa was saying now to Rachel as they wandered along the road by the beach. "I mean – suppose it's squid or something!"

"Mmm – delicious," said Rachel. "They call it Kalamari. It's fine as long as it's fried – kind of like onion rings. But – oh, look, Lisa, there's our supper!" She pointed to a quayside a little further down the road, where a cluster of fishing boats was moored. Next to them were huge nets with today's catch spread out and drying in the fading sunlight. There were lobsters, squid and a whole array of creatures with claws and pincers and terrible eyes.

Lisa looked appalled. "People eat that?" she asked, going slightly green.

"Oh, yes, these are the delicacies of the island," Rachel assured her. "And they're awfully proud of their seafood here. If you don't eat every single bit they get very upset. It's considered the height of bad manners."

"You're kidding!" Lisa said faintly. Then she looked more closely at Rachel and immediately relaxed. "You are kidding! You are rotten, Rachel. I just don't understand why I'm your friend. I'm not, probably. I think you just look very like a friend I used to have, and you happen to have the same name. I know, I bet the real Rachel Stanley got kidnapped by aliens and one of them, probably the most evil one, entered her body and is on earth now, sent to torment me with her constant irritating presence and her nasty jokes about octopuses."

Rachel looked concerned. "Oh, no — you weren't supposed to find out! I'll never make it back to my planet now. I'll have to carry on as a dumb, backward human, punished for giving away extraterrestrial secrets. Damn!"

The two friends happily carried on bantering all the way back to the Hotel Elena. Soon they were floating on lilos in the swimming pool, idly throwing a ball for some children, who would take it in turns to leap off the diving board to catch it, competing at the same time to see who could make the biggest splash.

"We really have landed a winner this time," sighed Lisa contentedly. "A beautiful Greek island, nice grown-up tourists for once. And, best of all, we're together again."

Rachel and Lisa had been best friends since primary school, and had become holiday reps together. They never knew where they'd be sent each season, nor even if they'd definitely find a contract. But so far they'd been very lucky. They'd worked together the previous summer in Spain, running a club for teenagers. And again in the winter, on a skiing holiday in Austria. After that, they'd both worked in London for a few months, Lisa at a fitness club as an aerobics teacher and Rachel at the Dream Ticket central office. Now, they were reps again, and to their joy they'd found work in the same resort – Linoka, on the island of Ephros.

"Oh, it's so good to be free again," Rachel murmured, remembering the humdrum days of word-processing, endless correspondence, complicated telephone bookings, faulty payments, while outside there was the constant drizzle from a miserable, grey sky. "I don't know how people can stick working in offices. I bet all those commuters crushed together on the Circle Line and stuck in front of stupid screens all day – I bet they wouldn't believe that you can get a job doing this."

"Yes, well, there are a few drawbacks," Lisa reminded her. "I mean, we've only been here three days and already I've had to deal with one lot of lost baggage, a bad case of sunburn and a mosquito allergy. Not to mention the Seashell Club!"

Rachel and Lisa had been indignant when they discovered that one of their duties was to run the children's club. They felt they were far too senior to do anything quite so menial as organize story times and clean up chocolatey mouths. After all, they'd run a whole teenage holiday by themselves the previous summer.

"Yes, well, take it or leave it," shrugged Janice Ingham. She was in charge of allocating venues for all the Dream Ticket reps and wore the constant look of a tortured martyr. In fact, she was a brilliant organizer, underneath her harassed, long-suffering manner. "You know I can never guarantee that you two girls will be together. You should be grateful, I must say, considering what happens when I do send you to the same place."

Rachel and Lisa looked shocked. "But we've always coped very well!" protested Rachel.

Janice tapped her gold pencil thoughtfully against her gold-winged spectacles. "Yes, that's true. You managed the clifftop rescue very bravely, I'll give you that. And the jewellery theft – cleverly solved, I'll admit. And let's not forget the poor young woman who nearly drowned when she fell through the ice. Most commendable, risking your life like that."

"Well then," said Rachel triumphantly. "How can you possibly doubt our ability to handle a crisis?"

"Oh, I don't, dear," said Janice in her very kindest voice. "I was merely referring to the fact that there do seem to be so very many more of them whenever you're together. Some would say I was foolhardy to try it again but that's me all over. A great big shiny heart of gold."

Rachel knew when she was beaten. Janice couldn't have made it clearer. If she and Lisa wanted to be together, they'd have to become Auntie Seashells and look after the kiddies. Embarrassing but true.

"At least it's only three days a week," Rachel said to Lisa, as they clambered out of the pool and made their way back to their apartment. "And in this heatwave, it's nice and cool."

"Oh, I know," agreed Lisa. "And look at everything else. Our own annexe, attached to the very nicest hotel in Linoka."

5

They had both fallen in love with the pretty Hotel Elena, run by the Ilyaki family. It was set a little further away from the town centre than the other hotels and apartments, with beautiful gardens, tennis courts and a lovely pool.

While Rachel was in the shower there was a knock on the door of the apartment. It was Alex, Lisa's boyfriend. They'd met the previous summer when he'd been a fellow rep and now they were together again. He had his own apartment upstairs, next door to the fourth rep, Alison.

Alex had changed since last summer. He was not as timid as he used to be, though he still had a slight diffidence about him – a nervous laugh, floppy hair drooping into his wide, surprised-looking eyes.

"Hi, I'm not dressed yet," Lisa greeted him – unnecessarily, since she was wrapped in a towel.

Alex grinned. "Don't apologize. That's just how I like you. Anything I can help you off with?"

Lisa threw her hairbrush at him. "Just you try!" she dared him.

Alex stepped towards her. She dodged him. He leapt across the bed to reach her. She dodged again, so that he went crashing to the floor.

Lisa rushed over to where he lay clutching his head. "Alex – Alex, are you OK?" Her voice sounded full of concern, but inside she was exasperated. Once, Alex and his clownish antics had made her feel tender and loving. Lately, she'd found herself reacting rather differently. It was difficult to admit, even to herself, but sometimes Alex really got on her nerves. Deep down, she was even beginning to wonder whether it was such a great idea for them to be so close together for the summer.

"Gotcha!" taunted Alex, pulling her down to him. "I win!" And then he was kissing her, his hands reaching beneath the towel and slithering up and down her back.

Responding to his touch, Lisa told herself not to be so ungrateful. She had to be the luckiest girl in the world to have such a wonderful, lovable boyfriend.

"Mmm – you are such a cheat..." Lisa murmured, sinking into his embrace.

"I know," said Alex, pulling her even closer. "That's what's so lovable about me."

It was getting dark now, the sun sinking into a glorious red and orange sky, as shadows settled over the mountains that towered over the little fishing village. The now familiar sound of Greek music, bouzoukis and violin straining against the melancholy dirge of a wailing singer, echoed from the taverna where Andy was cooking up his special barbecue. A delicious smell of onions and tomatoes over burning charcoal wafted from the yard.

Rachel leaned back in her chair, sipping a glass of retsina – a very strong, sour Greek wine which only tasted really wonderful when it was ice cold. The taverna was on a little hill right next to the beach. Fishing boats were getting ready to set sail for the night, lights were appearing all across the bay. All round her were the sounds and the smells

7

of holiday. And, best of all, any moment the man she loved would be at her side.

For now, though, she had to make do with Alex and Lisa, who were trying to throw olives into each other's open mouths. "Now try it with this!" Lisa said wickedly, picking a long green chilli pepper and aiming at Alex.

"No way!" he yelled, and then she was chasing him down on to the beach and right up to the water's edge.

"Do those two always behave as though they were in playgroup?" asked a cheerful voice behind her. It was Alison – the other rep. Rachel smiled at her – she was so easy-going and good-natured. And so determined to enjoy herself.

"Well, I suppose they do," admitted Rachel. "They're awfully fond of each other but they seem to show it in some very peculiar ways. Does it strike you as odd?"

Alison sat down and grabbed an olive. "It depends," she pronounced eventually. "It could mean one of two things, in my experience. Either they're madly in love but strange – which means they're well-suited. Or else they're putting on an act. I mean, maybe they've run out of things to say to each other so they play these games instead. It happens."

"How come you know so much about relationships?" asked Rachel, laughing.

Alison tapped her nose with her finger. "Don't push me. I just know. In my experience, the strangest people seem to end up together. I mean, really dull girls often land the most fanciable hunks. And then you get these fabulous girls who seem to prefer weeds and nerds. Oh, and then there's me, of course."

"Meaning?" asked Rachel.

"Haven't exactly ended up with anyone yet, but I'm really enjoying the journey," explained Alison. "My trouble is, I can look at practically any guy and think he might be the one. Look – over there, for example."

Rachel glanced over to a scruffy-looking boy sitting at another table, morosely gulping down a bottle of beer. He looked as though he hadn't shaved for at least a week, his hair was long and rather matted, his T-shirt torn.

"You see, a lot of women just wouldn't notice the potential in a guy like that, would they?" Alison whispered. "But I reckon with a bit of care and attention he'd polish up a treat. Here – watch."

Rachel gazed on, entranced, as Alison sauntered over to the guy's table and sat down with a winning smile. She chatted. He stared. She asked questions. He answered. Then stared again. Then the entire picture changed as a very beautiful girl in skin-tight jeans and a tiny bolero top appeared at the table and glared at Alison. The scruffy guy shrugged and Alison hurried back to Rachel.

"Oh, well – plenty more where he came from," she said, not the least bit chastened. "I was only demonstrating a theory."

A little speedboat whirled through the waves and landed, with a huge spray of foam, at the jetty where the fishing boats were moored.

Rachel pointed towards it meaningfully. "Well,

how about demonstrating your theory on him?" she suggested.

A dark, very tanned, very good-looking Greek guy had leapt from the boat and was sauntering up the beach towards them. Stavros was also a Dream Ticket rep, working with them but living across the bay with relatives. No one had got to know him very well yet, but all three girls had agreed that he was sensationally dishy.

So Rachel was surprised when Alison shook her head. "No – that's where I draw the line," she said. "Maybe I know he's out of my league. Or maybe he's just too perfect or something. But really and truly, he doesn't turn me on, Rachel. I think it's because I've got a sixth sense when it comes to trouble. And if ever I saw a bundle of walking trouble, here it comes now."

But Rachel had lost interest. Because while Stavros was making his way towards them from the beach, and Lisa and Alex were following, arm in arm, someone else was approaching from the other direction – a tall, handsome, quiet figure whose pace quickened as he caught sight of Rachel, and his face broke into a delighted smile.

"Jack! At last!" Rachel exclaimed, rising to greet him. It was just the briefest of hugs before he sat down with the others – but Rachel felt as though a fire had started inside her. Her cheeks were glowing, her eyes blazing, when everyone raised their glasses.

"To a successful summer!" announced Jack, for after all he was now their boss. Then he turned to her and added quietly, "And a summer of love."

As they all drained their glasses, Rachel reached under the table for Jack's hand. He squeezed it back, hard. Her eyes filled suddenly with tears. This was such a happy moment, so full of colour and excitement, yet for her it was tinged with sadness.

Rachel had been in love with Jack Woodford for a whole year, ever since they'd met in Spain. She'd hated him at first, especially as he'd been sent from Head Office to keep an eye on her and the other reps. Now, she was crazy about him. But Jack was rising fast in the Dream Ticket world. He'd been made Head of the Greek operation, working in Athens and looking after all the company's Greek holidays. He'd managed a few days on Ephros, checking out some of the newer hotels and possible new locations. He'd been away on the other side of the island since the day before. Now, though, he was about to go back to Athens. And this was to be their very last evening together.

But there wasn't much time to be sad. Andy's brilliant barbecue had arrived – plates were piled with unusual-looking charred fish, bright red tomatoes, skewers of meat, glistening onion... "I tell you, you have a treat tonight. So here eet ees!" announced Andy with a flourish. And then there was more chatter and laughter, glasses were filled, and the festive evening had begun.

Much, much later, Rachel and Jack wandered along the shoreline, hand in hand. The beach was deserted now, lit only by the eerie rays of the moon. When they reached the jetty, they sat on a rock, watching the last of the fishing fleet sailing out to sea.

"We always seem to be saying goodbye," Jack said at last to Rachel. "You'd think we'd be good at it by now, we've had so much practice." Then he took her in his arms and kissed her. A rush of desire spread through her like fire.

Without saying a word, he took her by the hand and they made their way back up the beach and along the road to the Hotel Elena. It was so dark that they stumbled as they stepped through the cactus garden, under the fig trees and up the stairs to the apartment.

As Jack covered Rachel's body with his and began to make love to her, he whispered over and over again: "I love you, Rachel – wherever you are. Wherever I am. You're the one – you're the one," until she felt she was drowning in his passion and tenderness and overwhelming, urgent need for her.

2

"We at Dream Ticket are here to ensure that you have the holiday of a lifetime," chanted Alison with a bright smile. It was the third time she'd been through the routine that morning and she was beginning to get bored. She and Stavros were hotel-hopping, as she called it. As it was the first weekend for the first batch of holiday-makers, the reps had to make sure they visited all their locations to make the guests feel at home; the Hotel Elena, where the reps stayed, a little away from the central square, and then a cluster of hotels and apartments further into town.

"As well as the lovely beaches we have a number of swimming pools at your disposal," Alison went on. "As Dream Ticket clients you are welcome to use the pools at all our hotels and apartment complexes. Water sports are available at various locations along the beach at a very good concession price."

Alison looked round encouragingly. Twenty pairs

of eyes looked back at her. No one said anything. Alison plunged on.

"Down in the town square, which is very conveniently situated a ten-minute walk from here, you will find a range of shops to suit your every need, including some lovely souvenirs as this part of the island is renowned for its jewellery-making. In the evening the square is a lively centre for night-life, with two discos and a whole number of tavernas. And, of course, at any time of day or night it's a perfect place to relax, have a coffee or a beer, and sit and watch the world go by."

Alison grinned but still no one spoke. She was not the least fazed. Tourists, she knew, were always amazingly quiet on the first day. It was as if they were in shock to begin with. They needed time to get used to their surroundings before they could start making trouble. She took a deep breath and carried on.

"This is a very lovely part of Greece and we at Dream Ticket very much hope that you will want to take advantage of our many cultural tours and trips which you will find are fantastic value for money and a great way to see the island. We are especially lucky to have on our staff a real, native Greek person. Stavros is dying to show off his beautiful birthplace, aren't you, Stavros?" At this, Stavros flashed a nervous smile round the room. "I know there are many wonderful stories that Stavros can tell you and he's also familiar with all the ways of the people here. So if you want to know about customs and traditions or if, for instance, you're having trouble with the currency,

Stavros is your man."

People did perk up just a little at this point. Someone asked whether you were expected to tip the waiters in restaurants. Another had a complicated question about traveller's cheques.

"Thanks a lot," Stavros muttered under his breath. "I get all the difficult questions, just because you had to go and mention money."

"Sorry," whispered Alison. "I was only trying to breathe a bit of life into them." She beamed round, suddenly remembering her patter.

"Oh, and I should mention that we have a very cosy and popular children's club — the Seashell Club, run by our very experienced team of play leaders. That's on Monday and Tuesday, two till four, and Thursday mornings, ten till twelve."

Several parents perked up at this information. Alison noticed a very attractive, bored-looking woman nudging her equally handsome husband, who had a blonde toddler on his lap. The two parents seemed to be disagreeing about something. He put his hand on her's, but she shook it off impatiently.

One to watch there, Alison told herself cheerfully. She answered a few more questions and then briskly got up. "That's about all you need to know, folks," she finished. "There's a notice-board here in the foyer with all the latest news, and one of us will be around every day, either in the morning or the afternoon. If you need us at any other time, drop into the office. Good luck, and happy holidays."

*   *   *

It could have been a playgroup anywhere, Rachel thought two days later, on Monday afternoon, as she surveyed the chaos of the Seashell Club in full swing. There was a large table littered with sticky paper and playdoh. Plastic bricks were scattered among dominoes, Barbie dolls and big wax crayons. And there was a deafening mixture of shrieks, bangs and the odd squeal as a dozen tiny children rushed round the room brandishing jelly, melting chocolate and sticky cakes.

The only signs that this was not any normal, drizzly English town were that the floor was cool marble, the children wore bright beach shorts and sandals and through the windows a brilliant sun scorched down from the dazzling blue sky.

"Come on, everyone," coaxed Lisa hopefully. "Let's all sing the Runaway Train."

"I'm the runaway train!" announced a small boy with red cheeks. "And I'm running after you!"

More squeals ensued as he chased two little girls round and round the table. Inevitably, one of them crashed into a chair and began to cry. Someone else was quietly being sick in the corner.

"I reckon the Hot Club was less trouble than this," Rachel muttered to Lisa, gazing round in horror at the chaos and mess. She was referring to the wild teenage club they'd run in Spain the previous year. "At least no one needed taking to the toilet."

"No, but there were definite similarities," Lisa replied as she raided the First Aid box for a plaster. "People were sick, hurt each other, cried a lot and misbehaved."

16

"I suppose I'm remembering the easy bits," agreed Rachel. "But still, what we need here is a system. I know, let's clear everyone up, calm them down and try to organize them a bit."

So between them, using all the training they'd acquired on all the other Dream Ticket holidays – though never before with children – Rachel and Lisa swiftly called the excited children to order and organized them into two groups in two different corners. Rachel took charge of the more active ones, promising them a game of splash forfeits if they helped to clear up the room first.

"It's a very good game," she assured them seriously. "In this bucket I've got a lot of forfeits written on pieces of paper. Each person has to choose one and do what the paper says. Then we fill the bucket with water. Everyone else judges you. If you don't do well enough we pour water all over you."

This suggestion was greeted with whoops of excitement, and the children busily rushed round, tidying up and putting things away. Then Rachel led her noisy troop to a little courtyard outside, while Lisa settled down with the younger, quieter group of under-fives to read them a story.

The little girl who had cut her knee on the table sat on her lap. "Is the plaster making your knee feel better, Maisie?" asked Lisa, cuddling her.

Maisie nodded and snuggled up closer. "Better," she agreed placidly. She was a very pretty, blonde child – easily the youngest of the five little ones. Lisa thought she couldn't be more than two. It seemed odd to her that her parents would want to leave such a young child in the Seashell Club. After all, she was little more than a toddler.

Lisa shrugged and turned her attention to the story book. The other four sat on the floor, eyes wide, thumbs in mouths, as she began to read.

She was still reading when parents began to appear to claim their offspring. By now, Maisie had fallen asleep, which Lisa thought just as well since whoever was collecting her was over fifteen minutes late and all the other children had gone.

Then Lisa was aware of a brief exchange outside the Seashell Club entrance and soon afterwards a flustered face appeared in the doorway. Her heart leapt. She couldn't help it. Standing before her was one of the dishiest-looking guys she had ever seen in her life. He was tall and thin without being too skinny and he had one of those velvety smiles that seemed to make his whole face glow. And his voice, when he spoke, was soft and caressing.

"I'm sorry – I'm really terribly sorry. I really didn't mean to be so late. Poor little Maisie..." He faltered as his eyes fell on the little girl, peacefully asleep in Lisa's arms. The young man's face softened.

"You angel!" he breathed. "You must be wonderful with children. I mean, she's not exactly difficult, but she's very little and she can be awfully shy. So you must have done wonders..."

Lisa said nothing. She couldn't. She was too busy staring at the gorgeous man's shoulders which rippled slightly under his denim shirt. She thought she could see a little chest hair peeping through the open neck. Not too much — just a taste.

"I'm not sure we should have left her all afternoon — not on her very first visit," Maisie's father went on. "I was going to pick her up much earlier than this, but things didn't exactly go according to plan."

Lisa pulled herself together. It was ridiculous, gazing at a complete stranger like this. She decided she'd better say something. "I didn't see you when Maisie arrived," she ventured. "Was it Maisie's mother who brought her?"

The gorgeous apparition nodded, rather to her disappointment. So Maisie did have two parents, then — him and, presumably, his wife. "Yes, Susan's very keen to have a bit of time to herself. I suppose it's understandable. She looks after her all day every day for the rest of the year. But it doesn't seem altogether right to me. I don't know — maybe it's my pride. I'd probably feel differently if she said she'd like to spend some time alone with me. But she doesn't..."

His voice had tailed away and again his eyes had fallen on his sleeping daughter. "Seems a pity to wake her, doesn't it," he said softly. "But you must forgive me. I had no right at all to start telling you my problems. My name's Martin, by the way. Martin Comely."

"Don't worry about that," Lisa reassured him. "Maisie's a lovely little girl and I think she had a good time. Oh, except for the accident." She told him about the bad knee and the plaster and he looked guilty all over again.

"It's all my fault," he moaned. "I really had planned to drop by earlier. Then it would never have happened. But Susan got horribly bitten by mosquitoes and she wanted me to go into town to buy some cream and it took much longer than I thought. And then when I finally got back to the hotel it turned out I'd got the wrong stuff."

He looked so sorry for himself that Lisa had to laugh. "Well, either your wife is very fussy or you are very useless," she teased him. At that point, Maisie woke up and rewarded her father with a dazzling smile. Then she turned to Lisa.

"Can I have a drink?" she demanded.

"Why don't we all have a drink?" suggested her father. "Let's go and have a Coke somewhere. It's the least I can do to make up to you for being so late."

On the way out of the club, Lisa said non-chalantly to Rachel, "Is it OK if you lock up? I'm just off for a quick drink."

Rachel glanced at the young man and the child, then at Lisa. "Now what are you playing at?" she sighed. "This isn't going to be one of your famous flings, is it?"

Lisa blushed. "Come off it, Rachel – he's *married*!"

"Exactly my point," retorted Rachel.

"It's just a friendly drink," insisted Lisa. "Look – he's here on holiday with his wife and his daughter and he wants to say thank you. That's all."

"So what shall I tell Alex?" Rachel asked meanly.

"There's nothing to tell," snapped Lisa impatiently. "I'll be back by six. I'll see you in the pool." And with that, she followed the tall, handsome figure and the little girl down the road towards the beach.

"So what are you doing tonight then, Stavros?" demanded Alison. They'd finally finished their morning visits and were lazing round the pool at the Hotel Elena.

"Nothing," said Stavros. He quickly got up and dived into the pool. Undeterred, Alison followed him. She'd meant what she'd said to Rachel. She didn't fancy Stavros, but she was intrigued by him and dying to know why he was so secretive.

"Nothing, eh? So where are you doing this nothing, then?" she asked, coming up for air just beside him.

"Nowhere. I mean – I have friends. I am meeting them in town."

"Ooh, great! Lots of lovely Greek men!" chortled Alison. "Can I come, please? I promise I won't sit next to you or anything."

"What do you mean?" Stavros asked crossly, unhappy at the interrogation.

"Oh, listen, sunshine, it's obvious you don't like people to get too close."

Irritated, Stavros made a lunge at her. "Oh, I don't know about that," he retorted. "I'm quite happy to get very close – for the purposes of shutting certain people up!" And, as good as his word, he grabbed her by the shoulders, ducked her under the water and held her there for a few seconds.

When she emerged she was gasping but

triumphant. "See, you do care after all!" she teased. "Honestly, you Mediterranean boys are so physical!"

"And you English girls are so pushy," drawled Stavros, grinning. "OK, Alison, I'll make a deal with you. Stop prying into my private life and maybe, if you're very good, I'll take you out one night to meet some Greek people."

A dark, good-looking Greek boy appeared at the bar at the side of the pool. "What's this, Stavros, you asking out one of the reps or what?"

This was Michael Ilyaki, son of the owners of the little hotel. It was the first year that they'd had a booking with an English tour company so the whole family was working hard to make the summer a success. Michael and his two sisters, Thea and Agnes, all helped their parents by taking their turns in the bar and the restaurant and doing chores like cleaning the pool and helping with the bedrooms.

"Don't you start," moaned Stavros. "All I want is a little peace. Alison here, she said she would like to meet some nice Greek boys, that's all."

"Well, be careful of his crowd, Alison," Michael warned her. "Nice – I'm not too sure. Maybe you come out with me instead, huh?"

Alison laughed delightedly. "The more the merrier," she agreed good-humouredly. Then she took a running leap off the diving board, spraying water all over Stavros, who responded by splashing her as vigorously as he could.

Don't fool me! Alison was thinking as they raced round the pool, squealing. *Either you're the coldest guy I've seen since that Christmas weekend in Lapland, or you've got something to hide. And I'm going to find out exactly what it is!*

3

Jack was sitting at his untidy, overcrowded desk staring fixedly at a computer screen filled with rows of tiny, indecipherable figures. A phone rang. Still staring at the screen, he grabbed it. He was about to speak when another phone rang. He grabbed that, too. Then a fax started to come through in one corner, and a buzzer went, insistently demanding his attention.

"Hello! Hang on!" he barked into one receiver. "Good morning, Jack Woodford here," he said into the other. Both callers started talking at once. Exasperated, he dealt with one as quickly as he could but by the time he turned to the second the line had gone dead. The buzzer was still ringing so he pressed a button.

"Yes, Jack Woodford here. What is it?"

"Call for you, Jack," said the office receptionist. "Are you free to take it?"

"Oh, why not?" snapped Jack. "I'm taking everything else round here. Hello? Hello? Jack Woodford!" he rapped out in a belligerent voice.

Then his voice softened. "Oh, hi! Rachel!" He leaned back, gazing out of the window at the hot, bustling street below. There was so much traffic you could actually see the fumes rising in the heavy, humid air of the city. Even the air-conditioning couldn't quite cope with the intense heat of the morning sun. Jack's shirt was sticking to his back and his hair coiled wetly round his face. But just hearing Rachel's voice made him feel calmer.

"No, of course I'm not angry," he said more gently. "It's just so hectic here. And I'd so very much rather be with you." As Rachel chattered on about the holiday-makers and the children's club, Jack sat back dreamily, listening. A sudden picture flashed before him of Rachel, tanned and relaxed, wearing those tiny red shorts that showed off her long legs. And then another image – of Rachel in his arms, her fingers raking his back as he crushed her to him in a wild embrace.

"Oh, God, I miss you so much!" he rasped, aching with longing for her. But then another phone began to ring, the computer started to make chiming noises as if to distract him, and there was a knock on the door. "Gotta go!" he said helplessly. "Listen, I'll call you. And I'll try to make it over next month, OK? Love you."

And then he was back in the chaos of the office, juggling the impossible rows of figures, dealing with crises in Corfu and muddles all over the Mediterranean.

There was a soft knock on his door as he was dealing with a particularly galling problem. "I told you never, never to let anyone in unless they had all the documents!" he was yelling down the phone to a rep in Crete. "That guy's obviously taken you for a ride. He's not a tourist, he's probably a cocaine dealer. Or a spy. I want you to get hold of his passport at the very least..."

His voice tailed away as he glanced up. In the doorway hovered a young woman wearing a very tight top, an even tighter short skirt and very, very high-heeled strappy silver sandals. He saw the tight top first. Then the rest. His eyes travelled up and down the curvy body, taking in her tanned legs, her long neck and, finally, the challenging pout on her full, red lips.

"Do it and get back to me!" he barked into the phone, then slammed it down, cleared his voice and looked up.

"Sorry to bother you," announced the vision in a breathy voice. "I thought I'd better introduce myself. I'm Mariella Porter – your new assistant?"

Jack stared at her, mesmerized, for a few seconds. "Oh, yes, of course," he said finally. "You're the reinforcements they promised to send two weeks ago! But they didn't tell me..." She was gazing back at him provocatively, one hand caressing the mass of blonde hair which was piled on top of her head.

"They didn't tell me your name," he finished lamely. Then he added more firmly: "Well, you're very welcome, Mariella, and I can promise you're not going to get bored. I'm snowed under here." He gestured towards the teetering piles of bookings and invoices.

Mariella smiled a slow, secret smile. "Snowing?

26

I don't think so," she drawled. "And I can assure you I have no intention of getting bored. In fact, I can safely say that neither of us is likely to be doing much yawning..."

"Coming for a swim later, Alex?" called an attractive girl draped in a brightly-coloured sarong. It was Thursday morning, and while Lisa and Rachel were on Seashell duty again, Alex had been sweltering behind a desk in a poky room in the town square. He'd just strolled outside for a few gulps of sunshine when the girls had spotted him.

"Oh, yes, Alex – do join us!" added her equally attractive friend. "Jenny and I are dying to get you alone for a bit of a splash." They both giggled, while Alex sighed.

"I'll see if I can get away," he promised. "But I'm on duty here all morning." The reps had to take it in turns to man the office in town, for two hours in the morning and one in the afternoon. Everyone hated it. It was hot and boring and usually involved nothing more exciting than taking bookings for various day excursions or clearing up problems with traveller's cheques.

But that wasn't why Alex was sighing. He was feeling hemmed in. That was the trouble. At first it had seemed such brilliant luck, landing a contract here in Linoka with Lisa. They'd both been looking forward to a whole summer together. But now that it was happening it didn't feel quite so exciting. Oh, Lisa was still the same pert, funny, affectionate, crazy girl he'd fallen in love

27

with the previous year. If anything, their relationship had grown deeper. And it was natural that
some of the gloss would wear off after all this
time, he reasoned with himself.

Yet he couldn't throw off the sense of unease
that seemed to constrict him these days. And
when two sexy girls like Jenny and Linda
sauntered by like that and gave him such an
obvious come-on, he was overcome with confusion.
He didn't really feel that tempted by them – they
were nothing like as attractive to him as Lisa. He
just wished he had the freedom to have fun with
them without feeling guilty or constrained.

Alex shrugged. That was the way it was, he
reckoned. You longed for the right girl to come
along so you wouldn't be lonely any more. Then,
the minute you made that commitment to her,
being single and free suddenly looked so much
more appealing. Especially when you were the rep
that everyone looked to for advice and guidance,
he thought, watching another pair of teenage girls
strolling past the open door. It was like being
offered the most delicious tea table full of cream
cakes and meringues, chocolate biscuits and
wobbly pink jellies – only to remember you were
on a strict, sugar-free diet.

"Oh, Alex – thank goodness you're here!" An
anxious-looking couple had appeared at the
counter, the man clutching his wallet. They
explained that they'd paid for drinks in a taverna
on the beach with a thousand-drachma note by
mistake – instead of just a hundred. "Alex, come
and explain we didn't understand the currency,"

begged the woman, practically in tears. "We can't go throwing money away like that."

Alex glanced at his watch. It was almost time to close up for the morning anyway. So he locked the door and followed the couple down to the beach. With his practised charm he talked to the waiter who had served them, then to the restaurant owner. "For you, Alex, we will pay them," said the owner at last. "It is just silly tourists, yes, no reason to believe them. But this time yes, because you say. Now let me give you a Coke."

The grateful couple bustled back to their sun loungers, delighted. Alex stood at the bar, chatting to the owner. Out of the corner of his eye he noticed a familiar bright red and orange shirt, and a halo of blonde curls. He glanced over and saw that yes, it was Lisa all right. But she was not alone.

Lisa was sitting opposite a guy Alex had noticed a few times at one of the hotels. He had a rather icy-looking wife and a little girl. But he wasn't with them now. And he looked anything but married. He was talking in a low, intense voice and Lisa was staring at him with those huge blue eyes, drinking in his every word.

As Alex gazed over at them he wondered idly what Lisa could possibly see in such a wally. Then he wondered why he wasn't feeling jealous – merely a little surprised. And then Lisa looked up and saw him. He was sure he detected a guilty start before she composed her face into a welcoming smile.

"Alex – over here!" She waved to him. "Come and join us!"

Alex shook his head and gave a short wave back at them, then swiftly left the bar and began striding up the beach, pretending not to hear Lisa calling after him.

When Rachel put the phone down after saying goodbye to Jack she felt empty and dissatisfied. All round her couples were walking hand in hand round the town square, or rubbing each other's backs with oil on the beach, or dancing together cheek to cheek, hip to hip, in the discos at night. It seemed so unfair that Jack was so far away from her when she loved him so much. She felt almost angry with him for not being there.

And it didn't help that Lisa was behaving so foolishly. Lucky Lisa had Alex there, right there beside her, practically living with her. And instead of just relaxing and enjoying the luxury she seemed to be intent on throwing it all away.

Rachel had been vaguely aware that Lisa and Alex seemed to be getting on each other's nerves a bit lately. But then, she told herself, they'd always teased each other, right from the very start. It was part of the way they were. And now that they were together all the time it wasn't really surprising that their good-natured banter occasionally turned to bickering. But still Rachel felt sure that something was wrong.

"Of course I love him," Lisa protested hotly when Rachel questioned her. "So we row occasionally? Who doesn't? It doesn't mean we don't love each other."

Then, just three days ago, after Lisa had eagerly

followed Martin out of the Seashell Club, Rachel had confronted her again. But again Lisa had denied that anything had changed.

"Honestly, Rachel — it's not as though there was anything going on between Martin and me. I mean, he's a married man, for heaven's sake. I just happen to enjoy his company, that's all."

"But what about Alex?" Rachel asked.

"Well, what about him?" Lisa demanded impatiently. "Alex and I are fine, so you can stop fussing about us."

Rachel had said nothing more but she knew her friend so well, she could tell there was something she was unhappy about — something she was hiding, maybe even from herself.

Lisa and Alex spent the next three evenings together and seemed perfectly settled — almost like a married couple who had got used to each other's ways. Then only today, after a morning session at the Seashell Club, Lisa had gone off with Martin again.

"Just a drink," she'd reassured Rachel. "Just a quick drink and I'll see you back at the hotel."

Rachel had returned to the hotel alone, angry with Lisa for flirting so blatantly with Martin. She sat at the bar by the swimming pool, watching a group of young teenagers splashing and diving and showing off to each other. If only Jack were here with her, she thought, sipping forlornly at her lemonade. She'd never treat him the way Lisa was treating Alex...

"Hey, what's up with you?" demanded a cheerful, unmistakably London voice. Rachel looked up, startled. At the next table was a very tanned, shiny-faced man in wildly colourful surfing shorts and a jaunty baseball cap. He was about to tuck into a huge plate of ice-cream piled with fruit and topped with nuts and cream. He grinned at her. "You don't want to go round looking so sad," he added. "Frightens the dolphins."

Rachel wanted to tell him to mind his own business but somehow he looked so funny that she couldn't help laughing.

"There aren't any dolphins," she answered.

"See what I mean," he retorted triumphantly. "You've gone and frightened them all away."

"It doesn't mention dolphins in any of the brochures," Rachel said. "And they're certainly not listed as one of the attractions of the Hotel Elena. I think someone else must have frightened them away a very long time ago."

"Well, I can show you dolphins if you like," offered the man. "I know these islands pretty well and there's this secret cove they like. I'll take you if you want. But naturally you have to cheer up first. Can't have them frightened off, you see."

Rachel laughed again and he proffered a large, firm hand. "Name's Gerald Birt," he introduced himself. "Pleased to meet you. I've been hoping to get to know you ever since I saw you swimming here the other day. Lovely stroke, if you don't mind my saying so."

Rachel wanted to mind, but found that she didn't. Gerald was so friendly and open that any rebuff would seem ill-natured. "I'm Rachel Stanley – I'm a Dream Ticket rep here on Ephros."

"I know," Gerald answered. She looked at him, surprised.

"I make it my business to find out about people who interest me," he explained. "Ever been to the Blue Mermaid taverna?"

Rachel shook her head, mystified.

"Funny that," Gerald commented. "I'm sure that's where I first heard you mentioned. I know who it was, my old mate Michael Ilyaki. Thinks ever so highly of you, he does. And I'm not surprised. If I was ever tempted to take an organized holiday, I wouldn't mind having you organize it. Not after what Mikey's bin tellin' me. You don't know how good you are, do you?"

"So you're not with a package yourself?" Rachel asked hastily, anxious to change the subject although she couldn't help being pleased by Gerald's flattery.

Gerald laughed. "Me? Oh, no, love. You'll find I'm a bit too independent for group travel. At least, I hope you will. Because there's a lot of things I want to find out about you."

4

"Alex! ALEX!" Lisa called after his retreating figure. But he didn't turn back, even though he must have heard her shrieking at him. Disconsolately, she trailed back to the table right on the edge of the beach where Martin was waiting for her.

"I don't think he heard me," Lisa said, worried. "Oh, dear, I hope he hasn't got the wrong idea about us..."

"And what would the wrong idea be?" asked Martin, looking at her earnestly.

"Oh, you know," Lisa shrugged. "He might think..."

"That I'm attracted to you because you're lovely and sexy and fun to be with," suggested Martin lightly. "What a ridiculous idea! I suppose he might really get it completely wrong and think that I was trying to get close to you because you're a sensitive person who really listens when you talk to them."

Lisa blushed, flattered but rather confused. "Don't talk like that, Martin," she demurred. "You know it's not like that. We had that one drink on Monday with Maisie after the Club. And now this one…"

"Yes, this one without Maisie, because I just happened to want to spend a little time getting to know you. That's why I took her back to the apartment after this morning's Club session. You must have realized."

Lisa faltered. "But you — you're married."

"Oh, yes — you don't need to remind me," Martin answered, a tinge of bitterness in his voice. "I'm married all right. But you've no idea what a relief it is to talk to a woman who isn't constantly complaining — who actually wants to know what I think about things for a change. I don't know how it happened, but ever since Maisie came along Susan's changed. She acts like everything's a huge effort — and she just doesn't seem to be interested in me at all…"

Lisa felt uncomfortable for a moment. Then Martin's handsome face creased into a smile. "But I didn't ask you for a drink to talk about my problems. I just wanted to get to know you a bit better. Tell you what, how about a game of jokari?"

He quickly paid the bill, then delved into his rucksack and produced two slim wooden bats and a little rubber ball. They made their way down to the edge of the water and soon they were concentrating on sending the ball flying back and forth. Lisa had slipped out of her T-shirt and shorts and was wearing a bikini. At one point she leapt wildly for the ball and managed to volley it back to Martin before plunging head first into the water. He rushed over to pull her up and then, both laughing hysterically, they waded further into the sea until Lisa was practically out of her depth. Then, still laughing, they carried on the game although every so often one of them would plunge into the waves trying to hit the ball.

Eventually, breathless with exertion and laughter, they panted back to the shore.

"Oh, you are a cruel, wanton woman!" exclaimed Martin. "I do believe you sent that ball all over the place just to watch me make a fool of myself."

"I don't think you need a ball to make you do that," answered Lisa. "But I did quite like beating you. Men always think they're so good at ball games."

"I think you're much, much better than me at all games," answered Martin. "And thanks, Lisa – I don't think I've had so much fun in ages."

"I'm glad someone round here is having fun," said an icy voice. They both started and looked up. A blonde, pretty woman in white shorts and a fresh, white T-shirt stood where Martin had left his rucksack. She was holding hands with a little blonde girl, exactly like her.

"Daddy!" exclaimed the little girl.

"Susan!" exclaimed Martin, recovering himself fast. "You know Lisa – from Dream Ticket."

"Lisa!" repeated Maisie happily. "'Lo Lisa!"

"Oh, I know Lisa," nodded Susan grimly. "Although it's possible she doesn't know you quite as well as I do. Martin, I need you to take care of Maisie while I go out. Is that OK? Or are you too busy having fun?" She stressed the last two words with heavy irony.

Martin sighed. "Sure – come to Daddy, darling." Quietly, he added, "But you could have gone out this morning while she was at the Seashell Club."

"I could, but I didn't," replied Susan. "You may have forgotten that we had planned to spend the morning together in the mountains. I waited, as a matter of fact."

Lisa stared from one to the other, horrified at the row that was unfolding in front of her. Martin looked defiant.

"I don't remember making that arrangement," he said. "And when I brought Maisie back from the Club you didn't mention it, either."

"No, I didn't," answered Susan coolly. "I found I was rather too angry to speak."

"Er, listen, why don't I take Maisie for a while and you two go and have some time together," Lisa offered eagerly.

"No!" they snapped together. She was secretly relieved. *Martin may be a gorgeous guy*, she thought, *but he's also married, and he's also trouble. Big trouble.*

"'Bye then," she said heartily. "Don't forget our barbecue supper on Saturday." She gathered her clothes and rushed up the beach without waiting for a reply.

The little jeep rattled alarmingly as Alex pressed down the accelerator and roared up the winding mountain road. Rachel sat beside him, her eyes tightly shut to avoid the view of the sheer drop on her right. "If we're going over the side just don't tell me!" she said between clenched teeth. "Just let it be quick."

"I told you, motor bikes are safer," commented Stavros from the back. "This island, it is not made for cars at all."

"But it was so nice of the Ilyakis to lend us the jeep," said Alison. "And besides, they wouldn't have one if it wasn't suitable for these roads, would they?"

"Maybe it's the driver who isn't right for the roads," suggested Lisa as the jeep bounced merrily over a pothole.

But Alex refused to rise to the bait. *"She'll be coming round the mountain when she comes!"* he sang. Soon everyone was joining in, even Stavros. They took it in turns to add more and more ridiculous verses to the old song.

"She'll be drinking Coca Cola when she comes!" sang Rachel.

"She'll be wearing Nike Air trainers when she comes!" added Lisa.

"Singing aye-aye-yippee-yippee-aye!" they all roared.

"Are you sure you know where we're heading?" Alex demanded after a while.

"Trust me," replied Stavros. "You are so impatient always. We are crossing a mountain, OK? The other side is a little way away. But I promise, it will be worth it."

He was right. They arrived at the lively little

town on the other side of the island just as the sun was sinking over the horizon. Lights twinkled and glittered all along the bay as the red sky faded into night. The town looked far busier than Linoka. All of them felt excited to be away from their little resort and all their responsibilities.

"It's not as if we needed to be around every single minute," Rachel had reasoned when they decided to have a night out together.

"Of course not," Lisa agreed vehemently. "They're all families, this lot, perfectly able to get along without us. We really only have to be around in the daytime, and for special events."

"Tonight – is for us, yes?" announced Stavros. He directed Alex through a maze of little back roads. Finally they tumbled out of the jeep and followed him to a low, brightly-lit building on the top of a cliff overlooking the ocean. The bar and dance floor were on the roof of the building, surrounded by a balcony where you could stand and watch the boats pulling out to sea.

"So who was that bloke chatting you up today by the pool?" demanded Alison, as soon as they'd sat down and ordered their drinks.

Rachel flushed a deep red. "It was hardly chatting up," she answered. "He was just a friendly guy, that's all."

"That's never all," snorted Alison.

"Well, this time it was," insisted Rachel. "Look, you saw him. He's at least thirty. I think he's going bald. He was wearing a baseball cap, which is always a sign with older men."

"Oh, yes – I know him," joined in Stavros. "You

are right. His hair is a bit thin on top. I noticed when I was on the top diving board. And he is a little podgy, yes?"

"Sounds like a real catch," added Alex, interested. "Did you say yes?"

"Mind your own business," snapped Rachel, remembering too late that nothing is more guaranteed to rouse the curiosity of well-meaning friends.

"Oh, come on, Rachel," they clamoured. "Are you going out with him?"

"You'd better not be," said Lisa darkly. "Whatever would Jack say?"

"Nothing, because there's nothing going on," sighed Rachel. "I told you, he's old, bald and podgy. But he's also here for the summer and quite good company, so from time to time I might actually find myself talking to him, as long as I have your permission, that is."

An old Beatles song started up and Alex took Lisa by the hand and led her on to the dance floor. "It's a long time since we had some fun," he said.

Lisa remembered guiltily Martin's words that afternoon — the very words that had led to his awful row with Susan. Suddenly she felt glad to be away from him and the heady guilt she'd felt that day, confronted by his wife. She smiled at Alex — a smile of deep affection. This was where she belonged, she decided. Here, with this sweet, funny man who always managed to look like a clockwork Dalek when he danced.

The music changed to a slow number. In Alex's arms, resting her head against his familiar shoulder, Lisa tried to tell herself that everything was all right again. Here she was with Alex, the boy she loved. There could never be anyone else.

"You're not drinking alcohol tonight, are you?" she murmured. Whenever she felt affectionate she found herself worrying about the man's health. Rachel was for ever teasing her about it. She said you could always tell when Lisa fancied someone because she'd start counting his calories and writing out diet sheets.

"No, but it's nice of you to be so concerned," said Alex.

"Well, I was concerned about all of us," Lisa replied. "Since you're driving us, I mean. But of course, I do think you need to take care of your liver. Haven't I always said you are what you eat?"

"Well, you must eat an awful lot of very fussy vegetables, I'd say," Alex teased her. "Because that's what you are. A fusspot. And I like it that way, I really do. I mean, what other man has his very own fitness expert watching over his breakfast? Every time I eat a bowl of muesli I feel grateful to you. I mean, who needs bacon sandwiches anyway?"

Lisa laughed, her arms tightening round his neck. There was no one like Alex, there really wasn't. "I never stopped you eating bacon sandwiches," she pointed out. "I just stopped you eating them every single day."

"Mm, yes – and you stopped me putting ketchup on them. You've always been so good to me." Then, after a pause, Alex added, "I hope you haven't been interfering with the eating habits of that Martin Comely. I'd hate to think of you forcing soy beans down his throat."

He'd meant it as a joke – a way of showing Lisa that he wasn't taking her little flirtation very seriously. But Lisa froze at once, furious with him for breaking their happy, intimate mood.

"For heaven's sake, Alex, why do you always have to go and spoil everything?" she fumed. "You know nothing happened with him."

"No, but I bet you wished it had," snapped Alex, stung by her sharp response. "I mean, the entire beach must have seen you making a fool of yourself with him this afternoon. I'd just hate you to get hurt, that's all."

"Don't be silly, Alex," she replied with as much dignity as she could. "I think we'd better change the subject, don't you?"

At that point the music changed again to a fast, beaty dance number. Alison grabbed Alex and began to snake round the room with him. Rachel joined in. Then Stavros moved gracefully on to the floor and pulled Lisa towards him. With surprising grace and ease he began to jive with her, spinning her round the dance floor in wilder and wilder acrobatics until the other dancers gave up and just stood and watched the two of them gyrating round the floor.

At the end of the number Stavros lifted her by the waist and swept her down through his legs, then twirled her up in the air and round and round as if she was a baton. Lisa had never danced before with anyone who combined such strength and energy with simple, fluid grace. As the room burst with applause and cheers she sank almost to the floor, shaken with the effort of the strenuous display.

Then the music changed again – this time to the relentless, sweet sound of bouzoukis and guitars. Stavros amazed them all again. He linked arms with five or six other men and began the slow, deliberate moves of a traditional Greek dance. Lisa, Rachel, Alex and Alison watched, mesmerized, as the men circled the floor, then began to move faster and faster, lower and lower as the music pounded into more and more complex patterns. Everyone was clapping in time and cheering on the line of men who were utterly caught up in the hypnotic rhythm of the dance.

They all clapped and cheered madly as the music ended, calling for more. This time, Stavros danced with two of the waiters – a far more delicate and artful dance which involved jumping over glasses of wine and waving handkerchiefs in the air. At the end of this one, Stavros beckoned to Alex.

"You will need to know this for the traditional evening on Saturday," he explained. "I show you now – then you can help all the clients."

"Oh, no," groaned Alex. "Why can't you do it?" But Stavros ignored him, and forced him to step sideways, bend his knees a little, then shuffle and skip as the music required. Alex looked so funny attempting to follow him that the others became helpless with laughter. Even Lisa forgot their argument.

"Alex," she called, still giggling. "Be careful!

You're going to pull a muscle, I just know you are. Especially after your leg."

She was referring to Alex's accident the previous winter, when he'd broken his leg skiing. Alex grinned at her broadly.

"I do believe you really care," he called back. "I'm almost tempted to pull something on purpose, just so that you'll be nice to me."

This, they both knew, was a truce – a signal that everything was back to normal, their differences forgotten.

But long after Alex had given her a long, passionate good-night kiss, Lisa lay awake, tormented by troubled thoughts of Martin's delicious eyes and gentle, confiding intimacy; Alex's ungainly jerks on the dance floor, his skinny shoulders and comical, open face; and, even more strangely, when she did fall into a fitful sleep her dreams were invaded by Stavros – his lithe, strong body gliding over the dance floor, swaying to the wild music and diving like an arrow into deep, deep blue water.

5

Rachel leaned back against the prow, her hand trailing in the water as the boat idled across the gentle waves. Gerald was lazily sipping from a can of beer, his other hand flicking the wheel occasionally to make sure they were on course.

"I love this boat," Rachel told him happily. "Especially the glass bottom. I've never even seen one of those before."

"Yeah, well, you should tell that company of yours to buy up a few," Gerald told her. "I couldn't believe it when you said Dream Ticket didn't even run its own water sports. You lot should wise up. Get your own boats and you'll be able to guarantee the clientele, won't you? It's a doddle."

Rachel stiffened at the implied criticism. "We prefer to give business to the local people," she said slightly haughtily. "Besides, what makes you so sure you know best?"

Gerald shrugged. "I just do know it. No point in pretending to be modest, is there?"

"I don't think you'd recognize modesty if it overturned this boat and snapped you up in its jaws!" retorted Rachel. But it was impossible to get really angry with Gerald. He was so funny — so self-centred and brash, and yet good-natured at the same time. Rachel had never met anyone quite like him before, and he fascinated her. That was partly why she'd agreed to come on this boat trip with him. The other reason was that today was her precious free Saturday and if he hadn't come to the rescue she'd be spending it all alone, feeling sorry for herself.

He chucked his can into a box on the deck and, with one finger still deftly guiding the boat, his other hand scrabbled in a bag on the seat next to him and brought out a very compact little cellphone. To Rachel's amazement, he started tapping in numbers and there, right there in the middle of the Aegean sea, the sun beating down and the fish leaping all round them, Gerald began rapping out complicated instructions to someone in a dingy office in London.

He seemed completely unaware of how incongruous he looked, sporting a loud Hawaiian shirt, a white naval cap perched on his head, while he talked loudly about orders and invoices and bulk deliveries and late consignments.

"What?" he asked, noticing Rachel's raised eyebrows and amused expression. "What's the problem? Wonderful thing, technology, isn't it? Here, you take the wheel a mo, love. I've gotta couple of tasks to prioritize."

Gerald then hauled a little leather case out of

the hold. It contained a tiny laptop computer which he balanced on his bare knees and proceeded to tap away at for twenty, then thirty minutes, his eyes furrowed in concentration.

"What exactly do you do?" Rachel asked, her curiosity roused.

Gerald shrugged again. "Oh, you know, bit of this, bit of that. I run a couple of businesses, sort of related to the travel industry. And property, in a way. But nothing that keeps me tied to some desk in an office." He fumbled in the ice box for another beer, squirted it open and raised the can to Rachel. "No, this is the life, mate. Long, hot summers, beautiful places, no hassle, no rush. And interesting people. Here's to you."

"Manage to see any dolphins, then?" asked Alison that evening, as they stood in the garden of the Hotel Elena waiting to welcome everyone to the traditional Greek evening.

"No — it's too hot for them," Rachel answered coolly. "They won't be back until October."

"Oh, poor you!" Alison exclaimed. "But then — some of us like it hot. How hot did it get for you, then?"

"Oh, really, Alison — leave it out!" Rachel said crossly. "I've told you, there's nothing going on between me and Gerald. How could there be? He's too old, he's not all that attractive and if you must know he's arrogant and bossy and completely without any manners at all."

"But apart from that, you quite fancy him," persisted Alison.

"Ooohh!" screeched Rachel in frustration. "Will you get it into your thick head once and for all I don't fancy him. I never have fancied him. I never will fancy him. I wouldn't get off with Gerald Birt if he was the last man on earth!"

"Evening," said a mild, familiar voice. Gerald had appeared from nowhere and was looming right behind them. Rachel flushed a deep scarlet. He must have heard her, she thought. Alison was guffawing so loudly that she was pretending to sneeze.

But Rachel needn't have worried. Instead of looking offended or hurt, Gerald took her by the arm and whispered: "I like your dress. It'd look great on my carpet."

Rachel swung round to glare at him full in the face, only to realize his eyes were twinkling. "Only joking, love," he said good-naturedly. "Here, come and sit down with me, have a drink, and I'll show you a trick."

"I'm not sure if I'm interested in your tricks," Rachel objected.

"Yes, you are," he told her confidently. As they sat down he fumbled in his pocket and produced her watch. He handed it back to her, reached behind her ear and pulled out an egg.

Rachel couldn't help giggling. "You're mad, you know that," she said, fascinated by him.

"You've got to laugh, haven't you?" Gerald replied equably. "Now, tell me all about how you're getting on with that book I lent you today." And to her amazement, Rachel found herself deep in conversation with him about the joys of crime novels, which she loved, and romance, which he admitted he devoured.

Suddenly, he seemed to tire of the conversation. He looked round, interestedly, as the tables began to fill and launched into one of his tirades.

"What are you doing, running your traditional Greek evening from this little place?" he demanded. "You'll never even meet your costs let alone get yourselves fluid. You could do with somewhere twice the size."

"We have a range of evenings planned," Rachel replied evenly, determined not to let him rile her. "Some are here in Ephros offering local colour without any travelling. Others will be more adventurous and, of course, more expensive."

"Daft!" Gerald shook his head pityingly. "All these opportunities for making a killing, and Dream Ticket is ignoring them. Oy, Maggi!" he called to Mrs Ilyaki, who was busying herself with the table settings. "How much you think you're going to make tonight, eh?"

Maggi looked up, too busy to take all that much notice of him. "I don't know, and if I did know I wouldn't tell you," she called. She seemed to treat him rather like a naughty boy who'd come to stay. "These people, Dream Ticket, they are nice, very good company. So don't go annoying them."

"Hmm, see what you mean," Alison whispered to Rachel. "He is a bit blunt, isn't he? Can't see what you see in him, myself."

"Well, that's exactly my point," Rachel answered, then realized Alison was teasing her. "So who've you got lined up for tonight?"

Alison winked wickedly at her. "Wrong question," she replied. "You should be asking, how many do I have lined up. Ever since Stavros let me meet some of his friends I've been having the time of my life. And there are at least three of them coming tonight. If you're very, very good I might lend you one."

Alison was wearing a tiny black dress with two thin straps over her tanned shoulders. Her hair was piled on top of her head in a multi-coloured scarf, and long silver hoops dangled from her ears.

"Wow!" whistled Alex, who'd just arrived. "You look good tonight, Allie. Is this all for me?"

"You'd be lucky!" scoffed Alison. "You're answered for. And besides, you're not Greek. But I'll tell you what, I think you're going to have to pretend to be. I don't see any sign of Stavros. So it looks like you'll be leader of all dancing and plate smashing tonight." And she laughed playfully as Alex groaned.

The restaurant was rapidly filling up with excited tourists, jostling at the trestle tables laden with barbecue food. There were families with children, clamouring for chips and complaining about the spicy tastes. Teenagers, anxious for the dancing, pretended they weren't with their parents at all. Young couples sat at little tables in the candlelight, their faces glowing from a few days in the sun.

After dinner the band was ready to begin. Lisa nudged Alex. "Go on – someone's got to get things started." She grinned encouragingly. "You'll be fine. You know how everyone loves you."

Alex made his way over to the microphone, lifted it off its stand, blew into it a couple of times and jumped at the loud, hissing sound it emitted back at him. "Oh, er – good evening ladies and gentlemen. And *kalispera*," he began nervously. "Tonight, as you know, is our traditional Saturday night Greek party here at the Hotel Elena. Thank you, Michael and Maggi, for your hospitality."

The Ilyakis smiled and nodded. Gerald turned to them and whispered loudly: "Hospitality is right, I'd say! The amount of food you've bin doling out you might as well be giving it away."

"Shut up, Gerald!" hissed Rachel, exasperated. "You'll give us all a bad name if you carry on like that."

"OK, OK," he replied, unperturbed. "I shouldn't complain – not with all this free wine washing around. I'll have another glass if I might."

"So who is going to join me to begin the dancing?" Alex was saying, trying to sound more confident than he felt. Lisa watched, worried for him. Alex was not the world's most graceful dancer, and now here he was leading the whole party.

Two of the Greek boys surrounding Alison immediately got up and each took one of Alex's arms. The music began, and the trio started to dance. The boys were so competent, so completely in charge, that they were able to make the dancing look wonderful – completely authentic. Everyone clapped in time and stamped their feet.

"Dance?" Gerald offered his arm to Rachel. He saw Alison sitting by herself and proffered his other arm to her. "That's it, girl," he said approvingly as she got up to join them. "Lovely girl like you wasn't made for sitting down."

"He's really nice," Alison whispered to Rachel, who was impressed by Gerald's easy charm. He just seemed able to get along with everyone. Rather to her surprise, he turned out to be a good dancer – graceful yet powerful, and with a real feeling for the rhythm and style of the music. Rachel found she was enjoying herself – it was good to have such an interesting, lively companion. And even better to feel so safe with him.

When the dance was over, several girls clamoured for Alex to teach them, too. "That looked too good to be true," Lisa remarked to Alison.

She grinned. "It was planned, I think. I mean, Stavros must have asked them to help Alex out – since he isn't here himself."

"No, I wonder where he is," Lisa said vaguely, remembering the extraordinary experience of jiving with Stavros, skimming and swirling in the air as though they had been one wild, ecstatic being. Then she turned her attention back to Alex, who was snaking round the dance floor in an ungainly, lurching march, with a whole line of people following him, all holding on to each other's hips. She felt a pang of pure love and affection for him. Alex was such a dear man – clumsy and a bit gauche maybe, but utterly kind and dependable and sweet.

There was a gentle tap on her shoulder. She swung round and came face to face with Martin. "Hi," he said quietly.

Lisa's heart jumped. She couldn't help it. He was such a good-looking guy, especially tonight, in those tight white jeans and a thin, silky shirt undone to reveal tufts of curling hair on his broad, tanned chest. And she just melted when his eyes held hers in that caressing, intimate gaze.

"I just wanted to apologize for the other day," Martin went on. "I'm really sorry about what happened. Susan was tired – not very well. She didn't mean to lay into you. Although she did very much mean to lay into me, actually."

"That's OK," Lisa said, embarrassed. "I'm sorry, too – if she thought there was, well, you know ... anything going on between us."

"Don't worry, I've explained all that," Martin reassured her.

"So where is she?" asked Lisa, her eyes darting round the crowded room.

"She couldn't come," Martin answered quickly. "Or at least, she didn't want to come. She's not feeling up to it. She said she'd stay at the apartment with Maisie. Of course I thought Maisie would enjoy all this, but oh, no, Susan always knows best."

"Let me know if he says his wife doesn't understand him," Alison whispered. "I'll come and kick him for you if you like. Didn't your mother warn you about guys like him? I think they should wear warning signs, myself."

Before Lisa could reply, Alison was on the dance floor, in the arms of a very dark, very handsome Greek boy who seemed to be teaching her some intricate new steps that involved putting his arms

53

round her waist and squeezing her against his chest. Alex was still encircled by adoring women begging him to dance with them. Rachel was laughing helplessly at Gerald, who was now attempting to balance a pile of plates on his head while dancing vigorously, talking non-stop and waving his arms in the air.

"The craziest Englishman I ever met," Maggi commented affectionately. "And believe me, I have seen a lot of crazy Englishmen."

"Just crazy about you, Maggi, that's all," panted Gerald, as several plates smashed to the floor. "Every time I taste your *dolmades* I dream up another plan to kill Michael so I can marry you myself."

Without saying any more, Martin took Lisa by the hand and led her on to the floor. They danced close together, his lips very close to her ear. "Lisa, I've missed you," he whispered. "I really would like to see you again."

Lisa pulled back and looked up at him in alarm. "Look, there's nothing to worry about. I wouldn't hurt you for the world," he went on, pleading. "Just a drink, and a talk... You're so good to talk to, Lisa, so good for me. Look. I'll bring Maisie to the Club on Tuesday and when I pick her up we can go to our bar."

They'd been there twice, Lisa thought. Yet he was calling it their bar, as though it really meant something to him. Why did he keep telling her there was no danger, nothing but innocent friendship, when everything about him seemed to be signalling his desire for her – that soft voice, words laced with meaning, those dark, velvety eyes boring into hers, the way he held her...

Then everyone surged back to their seats. It was time for the Ilyakis to take to the floor. Michael and his son, Michael, linked arms. They were joined by a third man, a cousin who was helping out that night. They began the hypnotic, rhythmic steps that were now so familiar to Lisa and Rachel that they linked arms and swayed to the repetitive, exotic tune. The music went faster and faster, the dancers more and more exuberant, until, urged on by the whole crowd, they began to dance on the tables, juggling plates and smashing them to the floor in a frenzy of abandon.

As soon as the sun had gone down that night, when the lights had started to twinkle in the trees of the Hotel Elena and the candles on the tables were flickering, Stavros had sneaked out of the back entrance and roared away on his motor bike.

He rode a little way along the rocky, winding mountain road that led to the other side of the island. Then he took a sharp turn to the left and was on another road completely – a road that led round to quite a different part of the island.

Soliniki was a busier, far more glamorous resort than Linoka. This was a place where rich Greek people chose to build their luxury holiday homes, near the long stretches of beach but not too far from the ritzy hotels and casinos. There was even a marina where they could dock their yachts.

It was at the moorings of one of these yachts that Stavros parked his bike. Glancing round him, just to make sure again that no one had followed, no one knew where he was, he made his way down the tow path, along the rope bridge and on to the deck of the *Rembetica*.

A blonde woman of indeterminate age emerged to meet him. Her dark tan contrasted sharply with her brilliant white palazzo pants and glittering T-shirt. Her ears, fingers, wrists and neck were all festooned with gold jewellery. In one hand she held a glass of champagne. The other reached out to Stavros, pulling him towards her in a tight, hungry embrace.

"Darling, it's been so long!" she murmured. "You've been so busy that you couldn't ring? You couldn't even let me know how you've been?"

And then Stavros was led firmly through the door that led down right inside the beautiful, stately boat, until he was completely swallowed up into another, very different, very secret world.

6

Business was slow on Tuesday afternoon at the Seashell Club. By four o'clock most of the children had gone, except for two little boys who were smearing each other with paint. Lisa was reading a story to Maisie who sat on her lap, sucking her thumb intently.

"Afternoon, ladies," called a familiar, cheery voice. Gerald's head peered round the door. "Another business triumph for Dream Ticket enterprises, I see," he commented, pointedly looking round the empty room.

"What do you want?" Rachel asked in her most bored voice. She'd discovered that the best way to deal with Gerald was to treat him like a spoilt toddler. It didn't seem to matter what she said, though, he never seemed to get insulted.

"Oh, I was in the area and just fancied popping in for a bit of company," he said vaguely. "You know how much I enjoy a natter with nice, bright girls like yourselves, and it doesn't look as if you're all that busy."

Furious, Lisa was about to tell Gerald to get lost. But at that moment Martin appeared looking flustered and ill at ease. "Well, maybe you're about to get busier," Gerald commented knowingly. He turned to Rachel: "Tell you what, darlin', when you're finished here why don't I take you out on the boat?"

Rachel shook her head. "Sorry, I've got some shopping to do. I need some new sandals which means going all the way to Palaki." This was the next town along the coast, bigger than Linoka and with far more shops.

"Tonight, then," coaxed Gerald. "Get your chores done now and then later on I'll show you the island at night. Go on, I won't hurt you."

Rachel was tempted. It was fun being with Gerald. He was rude and brash and very nosy, always asking her terribly personal questions. But he was terribly kind, and although he'd made it plain he was very fond of her, he'd never touched her, certainly never made a pass at her. And, somehow, she found that intriguing.

"Well, OK — if I can get everything organized," she demurred.

"Why don't you go off now?" suggested Lisa. "I can manage these last three kids and then lock up. Go on, Rachel — I'll meet you back at the Elena later."

Rachel glanced swiftly at Lisa's eager face. Martin was looking uncomfortable, shuffling from foot to foot as his little daughter scampered round his feet. Rachel could guess why they wanted her out of the way. But she told herself it was none of her business. Lisa could do what she liked – even if Martin was quite obviously an out and out prat.

"OK, thanks, Lisa," she said, making up her mind. "If you really don't mind, I think I will go." She turned to Gerald. "I'm on dinner duty until nine, so maybe we could go after that." And then she was gone, all three of them looking after her as though they'd been granted a reprieve.

"Best be off myself," said Gerald, watching her go. "I can see you two want to be left to yourselves."

"What a cheek!" expostulated Lisa when Gerald had departed. "That guy is really impossible. I don't know why Rachel bothers with him at all. How dare he talk to us like that?"

"But he's right, isn't he?" Martin said softly, gazing at her with those liquid eyes. "We do want to be alone, there's no denying it. Oh, Lisa, I can hardly bear to be away from you … I've been thinking about you all weekend. I didn't think I'd make it to Tuesday without seeing you…"

"Martin, you can't mean that," breathed Lisa, torn between horror and a delicious thrill of excitement. "You – you're married…"

"Don't you think I know that!" Martin rasped. "Lisa, I've tried to keep away from you and I can't. You're so sweet, so perfect, so good for me… Even if nothing can ever come of this, don't deny me the pleasure of being near you. Please…"

Before Lisa could reply they were interrupted by the clamouring voices of the last two mothers arriving to pick up their little boys. They'd been buying souvenirs together and were in high spirits, showing off all their bargains.

59

"Look, Lisa – this'd look lovely on you," said one, holding a shiny, sequinned T-shirt up against Lisa's shoulders. "And such great prices, too!"

"Yes, but you're not to tell my Dave how much I spent on this sarong," said her friend. "I know what he'll say when he sees it. He'll tell me he's not giving house room to an oversized dishcloth and if it's something to wear, why didn't I get one with the seams sewn up!"

At last, still laughing and joking, the two women swept up their happy but very grubby little boys and sauntered out of the club, leaving the door open so that Lisa could hear them chattering all the way down the street.

When they'd gone, Martin crouched down to where Lisa was sitting and took her hand. "I know what you're going to say," he murmured. "But don't say it yet, please – just be with me, let me get close to you."

Then he moved his face nearer and nearer until she could feel the quickening of his breath and his lips brushed hers. Lisa stiffened. This was too much, too fast – and somehow it all seemed far too calculating. She wondered how long Martin had been planning to get her alone and kiss her. Then she remembered Maisie and her alarm turned to anger. How could Martin even have thought of making a pass at her in front of his little girl?

With a jerk she pulled her head away from him, with such force that they overbalanced and both went crashing to the floor. "Sorry," Lisa said hastily, "But that should never have happened. And I just don't understand what you could have been thinking of – in front of your daughter..."

Her voice tailed away as she glanced round the room, first idly and then with some anxiety. Maisie was nowhere to be seen. Lisa got up and started to call her name. She rushed to the kitchen, expecting to see the little girl emerge with an ice lolly. But she wasn't there. Lisa checked the bathroom – no Maisie.

Meanwhile, dishevelled and flustered, Martin had hurried out to the front garden and down the road. Now he reappeared, running his fingers through his hair in despair. "The door!" he gasped. "The front door was open. Those women – they must have left the gate open, too. Lisa – she's gone! My baby girl – she must have wandered off and now she's gone!"

Afterwards, no one could agree on what had happened or how. All Lisa could work out was that it was a miracle she'd made it through the whole thing in one piece – and that it took a crisis to let you know who your real friends were.

Almost from the start it was clear that Martin was not going to turn out to be one of them. "What am I going to do?" he kept moaning distractedly. "My little girl! Do something, Lisa! You got me into this mess, now get me out of it."

Despite her own rising panic, Lisa found to her surprise that she was able to look at Martin quite coolly – and she didn't much like what she saw. How dare he blame her for what had happened? And how ineffectual he was, how self-centred he suddenly seemed.

"I think you'd better call the police," she said calmly. "Meanwhile I'll get over to the Dream Ticket office. Stavros might still be there, as he was on duty this afternoon. Between us, we'll have to scour the beach and the town and start searching in earnest."

At the door, she couldn't resist turning back to Martin to add, "Oh, and it might be a good idea to let Susan know what's going on."

At least he had the decency to flinch, she thought grimly, as she raced to the town square and burst through the door of the Dream Ticket office. Stavros answered after a few moments.

"OK, OK," he grumbled. "Take it easy. I was just about to close for the day." He looked up and saw the urgency on her face. "Lisa – what is it? Something is wrong?"

As Lisa poured out her story Stavros' face darkened. "This is unbelievable," he exclaimed angrily. "You say the child disappeared from the Seashell Club – from our own premises? That is very serious."

"Of course it's serious!" shouted Lisa. "She's two years old, for heaven's sake! She could be anywhere – with anyone."

"You're right, Lisa," Stavros replied. "Children do disappear. In Greece, it has happened that little children vanish – sometimes snatched away. But you understand what you have done? You have allowed this to happen to a child in your care – at the very place where people believe their children are safe. How could you let this happen?"

Lisa could hardly believe her ears. "Look, I

didn't exactly plan it!" she said. "And as it happens, she wasn't in my care at the time, not exactly. She was with her father, if you really want to know."

Stavros looked even more angry. "Ah, so that is why you were not looking after her," he snarled. "You were looking after the father, yes?"

"Oh, for heaven's sake," stormed Lisa, in despair. "Don't you start, Stavros. Nothing is going on between Martin and me. Especially not now. At this very moment he's calling the police and, I very much hope, they're about to mount a search party. Now would you like to quiz me about my love life all afternoon, or shall we help to find Maisie before she reaches voting age?"

Stavros' mood changed immediately and he looked contrite. "You're right, Lisa. I'm sorry – it was panic, I think. I will call Alex and Alison, see if they can join us. And I'll get together some reinforcements of my own."

Within a very short time everyone had gathered at the police station. Susan, looking white and drawn, was clinging to Martin's arm. He was doing his best to comfort her, and wouldn't meet Lisa's eye. She was overwhelmed with relief when Alex arrived and gave her a big hug.

"Don't worry, we'll find her," he whispered. "I know we will." And in that moment Lisa felt nothing but a deep, overflowing love for this kind, reliable, decent man who somehow always managed to make things come right for her.

Alison, too, squeezed her arm. "It'll be OK," she said. "I've been through this one before. Kids do wander off, and they're almost always found. You wait."

Lisa smiled at her gratefully. She wished Rachel was with them – Rachel was always strong in a crisis. But Rachel had disappeared off to Palaki and had no idea of the disaster that had hit them. By now, Stavros had rounded up a gang of half a dozen Greek friends, all with motor bikes.

The Chief of Police surveyed them sternly. He was obviously not impressed with anyone who could allow a little child to slip away from them without noticing. *Tourists*, he was plainly thinking. *More trouble than they're worth...* With a sigh, he began to direct the makeshift search parties. The motor bike gang were sent further afield. The reps were to scour the hotels and holiday apartments, and the usual haunts of the package tourists. His own group of police were despatched to the beaches and shops, accompanied by Martin and Susan.

"Do not worry too much," he added kindly to the distraught couple. "She will turn up. This is a very quiet little resort, we never have trouble. We will find your little girl."

But he was wrong. Two hours later the group had reassembled at an agreed meeting point on the beach near the town square – with nothing to report. The police were still searching, and Stavros' posse had not yet returned. Susan was quietly sobbing in Martin's arms. Alison was pacing up and down, pale and shaken. Lisa felt as though her world was falling apart. The only comfort was Alex, standing beside her, telling her that it was far too early to give up hope – there was plenty left to do.

By now it was early evening. Although the sun was still blazing down, the intense heat of the day had lifted. The beach was emptying now, with only the most determined bathers still splashing in the water, plus the occasional water-skier zooming past. It seemed that this nightmare had been going on for ever. Now, everyone was scanning the wide expanse of sand and sea, focusing eagerly on every child who wandered past them, only to have their dreams dashed again and again.

And then, suddenly, like a miracle, Rachel appeared. She was walking hand in hand by the sea with a little blonde girl, chattering happily to her. When she caught sight of the disconsolate little group she waved cheerily and began to make her way towards them. Maisie, spotting her parents, burst into a happy run. And then she was in her mother's arms, puzzled at why she was hugging her so hard and crying.

"Well, I wondered what on earth was going on," Rachel announced as she reached them. "I'd been ages in Palaki – you wouldn't believe how difficult it is to find comfortable sandals. And then, I found this great top—"

"Get on with it," urged Lisa impatiently. "It's Maisie we're interested in, not great tops. What colour?" she added, just to demonstrate her relief.

"Black and silver," answered Rachel, deliberately pausing for effect. "Anyway, I decided to walk home along the beach because the bus can take for ever and it's quite a nice walk really. You go past the little market and that nice café…"

"Get to the point!" shouted everyone. She grinned – and paused again.

"There isn't much more to tell you," she went on infuriatingly. "I spotted this little girl playing alone in the sand. She was awfully close to the water and I thought she looked very young to be by herself. And then I realized it was Maisie. So I brought her home."

"I can never thank you enough," Susan told her fervently, her arms still clasped tight round the little girl. "What we've been through this afternoon – all the terrible things I imagined…"

"It's OK," Rachel told her, embarrassed. "I had the feeling something wasn't quite right. Maisie didn't know where you were and she couldn't tell me how she got there, either. But that's quite usual with very little children, isn't it?"

"Well, maybe she doesn't know how she got there," Martin put in grimly. "But I intend to find out." And with that, the little family departed to the police station, leaving the four reps to try to unravel the mystery of that disastrous day.

Back at the Hotel Elena Maggi was serving them iced tea and clucking sympathetically at the awful story. "Thank heavens the little girl is found," she said over and over again. "But you must tell all your clients, no?"

Rachel nodded her agreement. "Maggi's right. There's bound to be all kinds of stories going round after this. And if we're not careful, it could look bad for Dream Ticket. Far better to put out the story ourselves – on the notice-boards."

"Are you sure?" Lisa asked miserably. "I feel bad enough already, letting Maisie out of my sight like that. But I never really thought people would blame Dream Ticket. It's just not fair!"

"Well, people do leave their children in our care," Rachel pointed out gently.

To Lisa's surprise and pleasure, it was Alex who came to her rescue. "Except in this case, the child was with her father," he said. "It may have happened when she was at the Club – but I don't see how Lisa or anyone else can be blamed, if her own father was there."

"Right," agreed Rachel. "But we have to make sure people know that. Then, I'm sure the whole thing will die down quite quickly and we'll be back to normal." Lisa looked so forlorn that Rachel felt sorry for her.

"Tell you what," she suggested. "Why don't you come for a ride round the island tonight with me and Gerald? You can all come – there's plenty of room, and he never minds."

"Not me," said Alison at once. "I've got a hot date with a gorgeous Greek."

There was a pause as Lisa glanced at Alex. He looked steadily back at her. "Er, no thanks, Rachel," she replied eventually. "I think Alex and I will stay here tonight. We've got things to do."

Alex nodded, grinning happily. "And besides," he added, "after all this excitement, I think we could do with an early night."

7

"Ladies and gentlemen, welcome aboard the *Fatima* – we hope you'll enjoy a very pleasant day in Turkey," announced Rachel, wearing her most efficient smile.

"Provided you don't eat the food, drink the water or buy any souvenirs," muttered Lisa. She hated doing the day trip to Turkey – she was convinced that it wasn't safe; it certainly wasn't very clean, and she didn't trust the food. Lisa was very health conscious.

"Ssh," hissed Rachel, trying not to giggle. "You're putting me off." She turned back to the expectant crowd who had gathered round her on deck. "Now I know that on the coach our guide, Abdul, told you a little about the customs and culture of this lovely country, so you'll know what to expect. There will be a little delay when we reach the port, as you will need visas. But then we should arrive at the town of Odili in time for a sumptuous lunch before going on to the antiquities."

"Which is quite a good description of the lunch," added Lisa under her breath.

"Stop it, Lisa," Rachel laughed. "I don't know why you've developed this obsession about Turkey. I really enjoy going there – and you get terrific commissions at the carpet factory if you can get people to spend their money."

"They'd have to be crazy, though, wouldn't they?" argued Lisa. "Fancy spending your holiday money on a carpet!"

"Oh, don't be so grouchy!" Rachel teased her affectionately. "Cheer up and I'll buy you some yoghurt with grapes."

"Big spender!" Lisa retorted. They grinned at each other happily. Rachel was relieved that everything was back to normal again, after the dreadful episode with Martin. She had been so cross with Lisa for flirting with a married man, even though she'd realized it was none of her business, as Lisa had been quick to point out.

"I know – I'm bossy and interfering and it's your life not mine," Rachel had admitted. "But you're my best friend, and I couldn't believe that you'd be taken in by such a corny line. Everyone knows about men who say their wives don't understand them."

"Well, as it happens, I agree with you," Lisa had confessed. "He was a slimeball, wasn't he? I should think the only thing he's really capable of having an affair with is the mirror! But I still don't think you have a right to tell me what to do."

"OK – I promise I won't," Rachel had said solemnly. "Provided you do things I approve of."

That had been over a week ago, and it seemed like far more. Now it was the next Wednesday and the first batch of holiday-makers had gone home, to be replaced by a new crowd. Most prominent among them was the Millington family. They'd never been abroad before and seemed determined to dislike it.

"'Ere, what's going on?" Tom Millington, the father, demanded as they stood in a sweltering queue at the Turkish passport control. "I don't see why we have to wait this long – we're coming in to spend our money, after all. You'd think they'd be pleased, wouldn't you? I've half a mind to go straight back again."

"Me, too," nodded his wife, Enid. "Dirty place if you ask me."

"Under outstanding characteristics on their passports, they should put 'champion moaners'," Rachel murmured to Lisa.

"They should get into the *Guinness Book of Records* as biggest fault-finders," agreed Lisa. "Still, there's always someone out to make the worst of it."

All the way through the long, tiring day, Rachel and Lisa smiled through the increasingly tetchy complaints of the Millingtons, who seemed determined to create an atmosphere of discontent among everyone on the trip.

"You don't expect me to eat this rubbish, do you?" Tom demanded loudly at the restaurant, thoroughly offending the manager who had obviously gone to a lot of trouble with the food.

"It's ever so greasy," agreed his wife. "All that

meat, looks as if it's been stewing in something unspeakable. And my children don't eat rice."

"Why can't we have some proper food?" whined one of the children. "We want chips! We want chips!"

"They want clobbering!" whispered Lisa to Rachel. But Rachel just beamed and explained the menu carefully to the family, suggesting dishes they might enjoy, while secretly wanting to spill the soup right into their laps.

Later, at the ancient monuments, which even Lisa thought were spectacular, the Millingtons were still dissatisfied. "Just a pile of rubble, this," commented Tom.

"It is over two thousand years old," Lisa pointed out. "This is the original site of a town, with its own theatre, and over there is where the hospital would have been."

"I know, I know all that," snapped Tom impatiently. "It says so. Doesn't mean I have to be impressed, does it? I mean, just a few stones – how do we know they're even genuine?"

"Well, this is just the entrance to the site," Lisa went on carefully. "If you want to see more, you have to climb that hill over there. The excavations have uncovered some marvellous things."

"What – all the way up there?" demanded Enid, horrified. "I couldn't get up there, not in this heat! Not with my legs!"

"We want ice-creams!" chanted their children. Lisa counted to ten and walked away, just as Rachel had always advised. Rachel was naturally impatient so she'd cultivated all these techniques for dealing with her temper. She called them the tools of the trade.

The girls were relieved when the fraught day was over and everyone had been herded back on to the *Fatima*, with no mishaps. No one had been abducted. No one had lost money or passports. Despite the efforts of the Millingtons, most people had enjoyed the day out and sat happily on deck, showing each other the jewellery and trinkets they'd bought in the market, and the boxes of sticky Turkish Delight. Someone, much to Rachel's joy, had even bought a carpet.

Soon they were approaching the glittering lights of Helios. In a few moments they'd be safely back in the coach. But just as Rachel was beginning to relax for the first time that day, a worried steward ushered her to the captain's cabin. "Ah, I think I should tell you, Miss Stanley," said the captain gravely. "We have a little problem. We cannot land."

"What!" exclaimed Rachel, sure he must be joking.

"I'm very sorry, but the officials at Helios are quite adamant," the captain went on. "They are worried about the cholera scare in Turkey."

"But that's ridiculous!" said Rachel. "The cholera scare is right down south, and in any case it's hardly an epidemic – just three cases so far."

"I know." The captain shook his head sadly. "You are right. There is no need for this, I think. But perhaps the authorities wish to make a point, no? Perhaps they prefer that rich English tourists spend their money in Greece, not in Turkey, yes?"

"Then why didn't they say so!" Rachel screeched, quite forgetting her rule about counting to ten to get over her temper before speaking. "Are you seriously trying to tell me we're going to be stuck here on this boat, waiting in the harbour, and they're not going to let us get off?"

The captain pursed his lips resignedly. "Well, maybe it won't be for long. They say they must have a doctor to inspect the passengers as they disembark. Everyone must walk over a disinfected mat, so the disease is not carried into Greece. They have already contacted the doctor, I think – so maybe it won't be such a big delay."

"I just hope you're right," Rachel muttered grimly. Then she braced herself to return to the deck and break the news to the tour party. This, she told herself, was the kind of moment when she suddenly remembered there were other, nicer, quieter, far better jobs back home. Oh, for a comfortable office and some boring paperwork!

"And further to your letter of the 16th," Jack was saying in a flat monotone, "I shall be happy to consider your claim as soon as you furnish my office with details of the cancellation and subsequent late charges."

Mariella perched on his desk, her legs crossed, as she took the letter he was dictating. Jack felt uncomfortable. She was sitting so close to him that he could look right down her low-cut, slinky top. He averted his eyes, but was nonetheless aware of her long, tanned, bare legs, her heady perfume, the pouting of her full lips as she finished the letter, then gazed at him.

"Anything else?" she asked in a husky voice.

"Er, no, that's all, thanks," Jack answered hastily. Then the phone rang and he answered it himself, relieved at the interruption. Mariella was gorgeous, there was no doubt about that. She was also very clearly available, and interested in him. And that was the trouble. The last thing he needed was involvement with another woman — let alone another woman who worked for him.

"Jack Woodford," he answered curtly.

"Jack, Theo here. Theo Ross." Jack sat up straighter and signalled for Mariella to leave the room. Theo Ross was one of the directors of Dream Ticket, based in London. But he'd had to fly in to Athens on business, and wanted to drop in for a chat.

Within an hour he'd arrived, and was pumping Jack's arm heartily. "Jack! Good to see you! How're things going?" Jack smiled, offered him a drink and filled him in on the latest transactions and problems in Athens, all the time wondering what he wanted — what he was doing there.

"Jack, I'm sorry this is such a flying visit," he explained. "No time for any in-depth meeting. But since I was here, I thought I'd come and check up on a couple of details. Oh, and one other thing."

Here it comes, thought Jack warily.

"We're thinking of making a few personnel changes," Theo announced, still beaming. "You know, shift a few people round, move off some of the more, er, traditional managers."

Trying to look relaxed and unruffled, Jack began to feel alarmed. Surely Theo wasn't going to get rid of him?

"Oh, don't worry," Theo went on as if he could read his mind. "We think you're doing a terrific job here – absolutely terrific. No, I just wanted to pick your brains about some of our reps. One in particular, actually. I've been hearing very good things about Rachel Stanley. Working over in Ephros at the moment. My sources tell me she's management material. I've seen her file and it's impressive, most impressive. So, what do you think?"

Jack looked steadily into Theo's eyes, trying to work out whether he was aware of their relationship at all. Was this some kind of test? There was no sign, though, and he wasn't going to mention it himself.

"Oh, she's quite outstanding," he assured Theo smoothly. "Reliable, calm in a crisis." He paused, remembering some of the crises. The clifftop rescue in Spain – when she'd been lowered by rope to an injured girl half-way down a precipice... Then, in Austria, her dramatic adventure over the icy lake to fish out someone who had fallen through into the freezing water...

"She's very organized, a good decision-maker... Oh, and enterprising, too." He smiled as he recalled their stormy first meeting, when he'd criticized her for not creating more commercial opportunities on her package. She'd certainly learned fast, he thought affectionately...

"Of course, she's very young," Theo was saying,

"and there have been rather a lot of, shall we say, events during her time with Dream Ticket."

"All of which she's handled with panache," Jack assured him loyally. "And don't forget, she's spent several months working with Janice in the office."

"Hmm, yes," Theo agreed. "Janice seems to be of the opinion that she has potential. And from what you're saying, you obviously agree."

"Yes, of course," Jack answered. Then added cautiously: "But naturally it depends what you have in mind."

"I was coming to that," Theo said. "As a matter of fact I was thinking of Marbella. Rachel's worked several times in Spain. Apparently she knows something of the language. What we have in mind is a position as Junior Manager for a year, starting in September."

Jack's heart lurched. September! Marbella! He made a quick calculation. His posting in Athens was due to finish at Christmas. Then he was coming back to London – and to Rachel. He felt trapped suddenly. Horribly trapped. Should he recommend Rachel for a promotion which would undoubtedly take her away from him, far away to the other side of Europe, for a whole year at least? Or should he try to stand in her way so that they could be together? And if he did that, and she ever found out, how much would she want to be with him anyway?

"Think about it, Jack," Theo advised. "I'd certainly value your opinion. You know the girl, you know the job. We won't act immediately. Ring me."

And he was gone, leaving Jack glaring gloomily into his computer, convinced that whatever he did now, he was bound to be making a huge, irrevocable mistake.

The boat had been in the dock for two hours and the Dream Ticket party was getting mutinous.

"Ridiculous, I call it!" fumed Tom Millington. "Stupid foreign nonsense. If it's cholera they're worried about then how on earth do they think they'll prevent it by getting us to walk over a mat?"

"It's just the regulations," Rachel sighed. "They have to obey them, and that's all there is to it."

"But I've seen two other boats who came in after us and they've been allowed to get off," objected a mild-mannered man. His wife murmured agreement.

"Yes, but they weren't coming from Turkey," Lisa explained.

"I've already explained," Rachel added, trying to sound patient. "They'll let us off as soon as the doctor arrives, but for some reason he hasn't shown up yet."

"I'm a doctor," offered one of the tourists wearily. "I'd be happy to supervise this charade."

"But they won't accept you," Lisa replied, on the verge of tears.

"Well, if you ask me, it's a disgrace," Tom Millington went on, making sure that as many people as possible could hear him. "Why can't you get another doctor, then? Call yourself a tour operator? My cat could organize a trip better than you. Dream Ticket? Nightmare Ticket, more like..."

Rachel agreed with him about one thing. This was like a nightmare. All round her, faces were strained and angry, children whimpering, the signs of misery and exhaustion manifest everywhere. And there seemed no chance of it ending, either. The Greek authorities had flatly refused to allow any of them to disembark. And they'd insisted that no ordinary doctor would do; the inspector would have to be registered by the harbour and approved by the immigration authorities.

Eventually, there was a flurry of activity on land. A thin carpet was unrolled along the jetty. Voices were raised, shouts exchanged. The doctor had arrived at last.

Still complaining vociferously, the exhausted party lined up and walked carefully along the carpet to the landing point. The doctor stood watching, swaying slightly.

"What's the matter with him?" Rachel asked the captain, who stood apologetically by her side.

"A little too much ouzo, I think," replied the captain sadly. "He has been in the taverna too long."

"No wonder no one could find him," commented Lisa.

"Oh, they should have been able to track him down," answered the captain. "He was in the Blue Mermaid – the bar where all the customs officials meet."

"The Blue Mermaid," repeated Rachel, frowning. "Where've I heard of that before? Is it well known? In the tourism books, I mean."

The captain shook his head. "No, I do not think so. It is for local people, really. But that is where I would have looked first. Strange, they took so long to think of it."

"Oh, I know," said Rachel, still thinking. "Gerald's mentioned it. He drinks there with his business associates. What a coincidence."

And then, as the last grumbling passengers were eventually on dry land, the two girls followed them along the strip of carpet, observed by the drunken doctor, and finally they collapsed, relieved and drained, into the coach that would take them along the winding mountain road back to Linoka, to the Hotel Elena and, they hoped, a nice cold bottle of retsina.

8

"So what's a nice girl like you doing in a place like this, anyway?"

"Oh, Gerald – do you have to be so corny?" Rachel teased. It was the following day and they were sitting at a table for two, overlooking the sea, sipping exotic blue cocktails in tall frosted glasses through elaborate, curly straws.

She glanced round at the pretty taverna and beyond that at the colourful market stalls that ran along the beach, selling jewellery, leather, beautiful shawls and locally-made silver. Below them was the marina, where fishing boats and fancy yachts nestled side by side in the glistening blue harbour. This was Soliniki, a busier and trendier resort than Linoka.

"Anyway," Rachel added, "I don't know what you mean by a place like this. Coming here was your idea, if I remember. You said you wanted to show me what Greek islands are really all about."

"And that's exactly my point," answered Gerald

triumphantly. "What I was getting at was, what are you doing slumming it with that two-bit little tour company, stuck in some quiet little desert just crying out for development that no one seems to have the sense to carry out?"

"I like Linoka," protested Rachel. "It's pretty and unspoilt, and at least when people come there they get to see a bit of Greek life. It's great for families, too. Not everyone wants non-stop discos and expensive restaurants, you know. What's the point of coming all the way to Greece for that?"

"Money, that's the point," Gerald replied simply. "That's what the travel business is all about, isn't it? You take people on holidays in order to make money out of them."

"That's not quite how I like to see it," Rachel answered huffily.

"Maybe not, but it's true all the same." Gerald looked at her intently. "I've been watching you, you know. You're good, Rachel. Very good. Probably too good for such a small operation. I mean, a proper company could make a killing over here. Linoka's ripe for it – but all you've got are a few apartments and a couple of two-star hotels."

"But it's affordable," Rachel pointed out, trying not to sound too much like Janice Ingham. "Middle-range family holidays offering comfort without luxury."

"Amateurs," scoffed Gerald. "You know what you need? Gourmet restaurants, water sport concessions, helicopter trips round the island, for starters."

"I don't know why I bother spending time with

you," Rachel said crossly. "You're rude and bossy and greedy and vulgar."

"That's my charm," Gerald grinned. "I know my own mind and I know what I like. Which is probably why we get on so well. We're both definite sort of people, aren't we? And we're both winners."

"Are we?" Rachel asked, intrigued.

"Come off it – it shows a mile off," Gerald told her. "You're the kind of girl who knows what she wants and goes for it. You're going to go far, girl. Success, that's what you're made of."

Rachel was flattered and rather baffled, as she usually was in Gerald's company. He was capable of infuriating her one moment, then suddenly, disarmingly, making her laugh, or complimenting her. He seemed genuinely to enjoy her company. But he never made a pass at her, never even touched her. She just couldn't make out quite what he wanted.

"Say cheese!" Gerald urged suddenly. He'd produced a tiny, bright green camera and now snapped a picture of her, then another and another in very quick succession.

"You're treating that thing like a machine gun," Rachel laughed.

Gerald looked pleased. "Like it? It's new. I don't just mean new to me. It's new on the market. Got it from a mate in the business. Look at what it can do!" He came round to sit next to her, placed the camera on the table and pressed a button. Then he put an arm round her and grinned. The camera obediently clicked, then clicked again. "Clever, innit?" Gerald beamed, just like a little boy with a new toy.

After their drink, they clambered back into his boat and rode round the island back to Linoka. Maggi and Michael were sitting by the pool eating a delicious-looking salad laced with olives and chillis.

"Hallo, mates!" exclaimed Gerald. "We don't often get the pleasure of seeing you two together. Let alone enjoying yourselves. You work too hard, you know, you really do."

Michael smiled tolerantly. "You wouldn't understand," he told him. "Here, we are brought up to work hard. Not like you – I can tell you are a rich man, but also a lazy one. You are, what they say – a fat cat."

Rachel thought Gerald might be offended. He did have the beginnings of a paunch. But he just roared with delighted laughter. "Not that rich, but probably lazy," he said. "But I can't see the virtue in working hard if you don't need to." He called over Michael's daughter Thea who was serving at the bar, and ordered retsina wine for all of them.

"You're a good family, a lovely family," Gerald went on in his normal direct, affable tone. "You run a lovely place. But why not hire more help, give yourselves a break. I could show you how, if you like."

"Oh, no, you couldn't," Rachel intervened, exasperated at him for his brashness. After all, the Ilyakis were contracted to Dream Ticket. If anyone was going to help them with the business, it was them, not Gerald.

But Michael and Maggi just smiled knowingly at each other and sighed. "I do not want your help," Michael explained gently. "This is the way we are here on Ephros. We work hard, very hard. But then we appreciate our rest. These moments are precious. Then, I have my music – I love to listen to my Greek music. And we love to eat, to drink, to dance. All these things we do well, very well, because we have earned them. By hard, hard work."

"Very nice," commented Gerald. "Very sweet. But you could be making more money, couldn't you, and then you could have more parties, more time off."

Rachel laughed. "Don't listen to him! He'll never understand people who are contented. He thinks everyone should be driven and dissatisfied like he is."

"Too right, I do," Gerald agreed. "Because that's what success is all about. Now take your hotel."

"Oh, no, not again," laughed Michael. "How many times do we have to tell you? We like it the way it is. We have a good way of life. We are happy."

"But wait," demurred Maggi, who had been listening carefully to the conversation. "Let us hear what he has to say. We don't want to refuse to hear good ideas, do we? Not if they could make us a little more…"

"Well, take your facilities, for a start," Gerald began. "Those little showers are no good – no good at all. Not for today's market. What you want are power showers. That's what discerning tourists are looking for. A bit of comfort. Put in a better class of plumbing and you can put your prices up."

"But Dream Ticket, they tell us —" began Maggi anxiously.

"Yes, we did," Rachel said firmly. "We advised the hotel not to upgrade the showers because we at Dream Ticket have a deep respect for the environment and the local people. We don't want to be the kind of company who storms into some beautiful, far-away place like a marauding army and plunders all its natural resources in order to make the rich conquerors more comfortable and more powerful."

"Ooh, get her!" taunted Gerald. "You may sound all high and mighty, but like I keep telling you, you're in the travel business. And what you just described is exactly what the travel business does."

"Not necessarily," Rachel retorted hotly. "You look out there – just down the road. Look at the parched, yellow fields. They don't have enough water, Gerald. I've watched people working in those fields. I've even met some of the farmers. The more water we pump in for the tourists, the more we are likely to damage local agriculture. You have to strike a balance."

Gerald shrugged. "Fine words – but how do you feel about it?" He addressed the Ilyakis, who were listening quietly. "You want to make your hotel a success? Or you want to keep it modest, and work yourselves to the bone, knowing that you could be earning more?"

"I'm happy the way we are," Michael answered at once. "Rachel, she's right. We do not want our island spoiled. We want our visitors to enjoy it without damaging it. This is best, I think."

Maggi looked less certain. "I am not in love with hard work, like my husband," she said slowly. "But too much change is a worry. We are best doing what we know, the way we know it."

"Up to you, obviously," Gerald answered. "And very nice it is too. Don't get me wrong. But if you ever want advice about upgrading, I'm your man. Now then," he turned to Rachel. "I want you to tell me all about this top you're wearing."

Rachel was amazed, as she always was, at his ability to switch subjects so suddenly, and to launch into anything at all with such vibrant curiosity and energy. She was wearing a very soft, silky, flame-coloured T-shirt dotted with glittering flowers. Gerald wanted to know where she'd bought it, how much it had cost, whether it was considered very fashionable.

"It's a new fabric, isn't it?" he asked. "Some sort of micro-fibre that clings to your body without getting creased."

He managed to say it without sounding the least bit suggestive. Rachel felt almost offended. "I thought you were going to say it really suited me," she said. "Especially with my tan."

"Oh, yeah, yeah, course it does," Gerald said vaguely. "You're gorgeous, doll, you know you are. Only, I was interested because a mate of mine is into fashion and he's told me a bit about these new textiles. They're ever so cheap. You can make a fortune."

"Is that all you're interested in?" asked Rachel.

"Yes," Gerald answered. "I like money. I like spending it. And I like you."

Alex knocked gingerly on the door of the apartment, which was part of the complex of rooms round the Hotel Elena. He hated it when there were problems with the accommodation. People always assumed he'd be able to fix things. It was so embarrassing. Once, he'd created havoc by reporting a power cut when in fact it was simply a fuse that needed replacing. Another time, he'd managed to break a wardrobe chasing a particularly nasty insect with a squash racquet.

Now, having been summoned by the emergency buzzer, he had no idea what the complaint would be. He usually hoped for something major, something that would definitely involve experts. It was the little problems like stiff doorknobs and toilets that wouldn't flush which really bothered him because everyone thought he'd just walk in with a bag of tools and make everything better.

The door was answered by a very tall, very tanned, very blonde girl wearing nothing but a towel. Alex wondered whether he was dreaming. Then he remembered – this was Astrid, one of a party of four girls from Holland who had booked their holiday through Dream Ticket. It was a new deal – usually the company just handled British tours. But now they were branching out. Staring at the beautiful, dripping woman, Alex decided it was a very good business development. Very good indeed.

"Oh, hello," Astrid said, her face lighting up

with a smile of relief. "Thank you for coming. I am so pleased to see you. I am having a problem with the tip."

"With the tip of what?" Alex asked stupidly, unable to take his eyes off her.

"No, not the tip," Astrid broke into a peal of laughter. "I said the top!"

"The top of what?" Alex repeated, baffled. "Do you mean the ceiling? Or the roof? Or maybe you're talking about your head... Although I can't see any particular problem there. Oh, yes, I can. You've got shampoo all over it. Did you know?"

Astrid was now helpless with giggles. "You are teasing me, no?" she said. "You laugh at my English. I'd just like to see you talking Dutch."

"I'm sorry, I didn't mean to offend you," Alex said as he walked into the apartment. Nothing appeared to be wrong there. He peered round the door to the tiny bathroom and saw footprints leading from the shower. He looked back at Astrid, her hair soapy, her shoulders still wet. That was when the light dawned.

"Oh, you mean tap!" he said. "You can't get the tap to work?"

"Exactly!" Astrid beamed. "I was having my shower and washing my hair. Then, suddenly, the water went drip, drip, drip – then nothing. I hope you can fix, yes? Because I need to finish – the soap is not good to leave in the hair."

Alex, trying to look efficient and knowledgeable, tried the shower tap. It didn't respond. He tried the basin tap. Nothing. "Hang on – I'll be back!" he called, and left.

He was back within minutes, bearing four large bottles of mineral water. "My water doesn't seem to be working either," he told her cheerfully. "But I couldn't just leave you in the lurch with soap in your hair. So I've brought you these."

Astrid stared at him as though he was mad. "But Alex – this is fizzy water!"

"So?" Alex said briskly. "It'll be fine – I promise."

So Alex found himself standing in the doorway watching this beautiful, blonde girl wearing nothing but a towel, who was bending over the basin, pouring bottle after bottle of cold, fizzy water over her head.

But very soon his reverie was interrupted by a loud commotion outside, and the clamour of raised voices. With a sigh, he forced himself away from Astrid. "I think there's trouble out there," he mumbled. "Better go."

Outside, a crowd of people was gathering, some bearing buckets, others looking mutinous. Rachel appeared, bearing two huge urns. "What's going on?" Alex asked.

Rachel looked grim. "Water crisis. The plumbing in the hotel and the apartments round it has all gone wrong. I just can't understand it – it's been fine up till now."

Maggi Ilyaki appeared, her face creased in worried frowns. "I think maybe our system is too weak for such heavy use," she said. "You know, this is the first year we have so many people. The annexe here –" she pointed to Astrid's building – "we have only just built it. Because of the new contract with Dream Ticket, we thought we'd manage the extra guests. But the plumbing is not strong enough."

"What did I tell you, Mrs Ilyaki – what was I saying only this afternoon?" This was Gerald, strutting complacently out into the evening sun to watch the havoc. "I knew you'd come round to my way of thinking, in the end."

"Oh, do shut it!" fumed Rachel. "You're glad this is happening, aren't you?" She turned to Maggi. "Listen, I'm sure this is just a temporary hiccup, isn't it? You're worrying too much – everyone gets the odd water cut over here."

Maggi nodded uncertainly. "Yes, it is true. But it has not happened so far this year. I thought we would be OK. Maybe you're right – but I wish we had installed something a little more sophisticated."

"Quite right!" approved Gerald. "But since you didn't, why don't we just form a line to the well and help everyone to get enough water for this evening?"

Rachel stared at him, infuriated and grateful at the same time. One minute he seemed almost to be rejoicing in their misfortune. Now, suddenly, he was earnestly helpful, organizing everyone into water-drawing teams, and pumping away vigorously at the little well in the hotel garden which they used for emergencies.

"This is all we needed," murmured Lisa, who had just arrived back from her stint at the club office. "Another reason for this lot to start moaning."

"I know," agreed Rachel. "And another reason

for them all to start blaming Dream Ticket for every little thing in their lives that doesn't go exactly according to plan!"

9

"So, who feels like dancing?" enquired Stavros. No one looked up. No one felt much like having fun. It was later that evening. The reps had spent an uncomfortable couple of hours coping with the water shortage and, more tricky still, with the moans and complaints of the clientele of the Hotel Elena. Now they were sitting slumped on Rachel's balcony, sipping coffee and trying to relax.

"It's as if it was our fault," complained Lisa. "Like we'd gone and turned off the water supply on purpose, just for a laugh."

"At least it was only the Hotel Elena," Alex pointed out. "Imagine what would have happened if all our properties had run dry at the same time."

"Don't," shuddered Alison. "This was bad enough. But think about those four-storey apartments downtown! Our legs would have dropped off!"

"My arms are worn out," wailed Rachel. "All that pumping and lifting! I suppose it's good, really, to remember what the people who live here have to go through. I don't suppose they've had running water all that long. You forget what a luxury it is."

Lisa giggled. "Were your arms worn out when you spilt that whole bucketful all over Tom Mullington and his horrible kids?"

"Partly." Rachel grinned. "It was a sort of accident, but I wasn't all that sorry."

Lisa got up and stood at the balcony, holding on to the railing. "Better do a bit of stretching," she explained. "You can put your back out if you do too much lifting." She began to bend down, legs apart, in a kind of squat, breathing out in a loud whoosh as she did so. Then up, very steadily, then down again with another whoosh.

"Cut it out, will you?" snapped Alex irritably. "You sound like a steam train with asthma. It's like listening to a hospital full of old men with pneumonia." He hated himself the moment the words were uttered. Lisa looked so hurt. Her face reddened and she rushed inside, banged out of Rachel's room and into her own with another slam of the door.

Alex didn't go after her, despite Rachel's surprised, accusing look. His memory was too full of the extraordinary encounter with Astrid. He could still feel the tingling sensation of her nearness, the softness of her skin, her lithe, graceful movements, her body beneath the thin, wet towel. How could he help comparing her slow sensuality with Lisa's quick, nervous energy – her natural grace with Lisa's sporty bounciness?

Stavros stared at him steadily for a moment or two. Then shrugged and repeated: "So, anyone for a night out? I think it would do us good, yes?"

"I wouldn't mind, actually," said Alison. "We certainly could do with a bit of fun. Anyone else?" Rachel and Alex were silent. "I think I'll go and ask Lisa, then," Alison went on.

She left the room followed, surprisingly, by Stavros. When Lisa opened the door to them it was plain she'd been crying, but she smiled bravely. "Come on, Lisa – let's go and rave it up a bit!" Alison urged.

Stavros added, "You might enjoy it, you know. Alison has been nagging me to show her some real Greek night-life. So tonight, there is a little party. My friend is picking me up in his jeep at nine o'clock. You come and have a good time, yes? Maybe have a dance."

There was a shuffling noise behind them. Alex had appeared, looking sheepish. The others disappeared tactfully as he entered the room.

"I'm sorry, Lisa," he muttered. "I don't know what got into me, talking to you like that. It was horrible and I didn't mean it."

Lisa looked at him sadly. "Didn't you?" she asked quietly. "Listen, Alex, what you said didn't matter at all. You've said far worse things in the past, and it's been fine. What was different this time was that you seemed to want to hurt me. It was like being hit."

Alex sighed. "I know," he admitted. "I know

what you mean — but I am sorry, really. Look — come here."

And then she was in his arms, and as their lips pressed gently together and he pulled her close to him, he was willing the old sweet magic to return. "I don't know what's been going wrong, lately," he whispered. "But let's not let it, OK?"

"Do you mean that?" Lisa asked, looking up into his eyes.

He nodded. "I don't want us to split up, do you?"

Lisa shook her head. "No, I think we've got too much going for us."

"Maybe we've just been through a bad patch," agreed Alex. "Lots of couples do, don't they? But we've been so happy, we didn't see it coming."

Lisa smiled affectionately at him. "I do love you, Alex," she said, meaning it.

"I love you too," he replied. And then they were kissing again, both pushing aside their doubts in an effort to make their love work again.

There was a banging at the door. "So — you two coming partying?" demanded Stavros. They looked at each other and giggled.

"Er, no," called Lisa. "We're going to stay here. I think we both need an early night."

The party was at a very large, very splendid house up in the mountains. Stavros' friend Chris flashed his headlights to activate the electronic gates. They parted to reveal an impressive drive-way flanked with cacti; and exotic fountains cascading down brightly-lit rocks into glittering pools laden with lilies.

Rachel was impressed, and began to think that maybe she would enjoy the evening after all. She hadn't wanted to come. She was depressed after the water crisis – and even more depressed at the tension between Alex and Lisa. Why couldn't those two just enjoy being together? she wondered jealously. She'd have done anything to be with Jack for a day, let alone a whole summer.

But Alison and Stavros had coaxed her into coming along with them so good-naturedly that it had been impossible to refuse. And now, as they scrambled out of the jeep and made their way into the lavish house, she had to admit she was glad they'd persuaded her.

They made their way through a vast marble-floored hallway flanked with valuable-looking statues, into a huge room packed with people. A trestle table groaned with huge trays of food while waiters handed round drinks and refilled glasses. The room opened onto a large garden dotted with candlelit tables, and overlooking a huge, floodlit swimming pool.

Alison seemed to disappear at once into the mêlée. Rachel saw Stavros deep in conversation with a couple of very well-dressed women, dripping with jewellery, and their escorts, a good deal older and wearing dinner suits.

"Say I've been busy," Stavros was saying urgently to them. "Just send my love, say I've had a lot on at work. I'll be over as soon as I can. Yes – I know. I know."

"Fancy friends you hang out with," Rachel commented as he stalked past her.

He glared at her, then softened. "Oh, they're friends of my – er, my mother. You know what mothers are like. If you phone, they say why didn't you ring yesterday. If you visit, they say you don't visit enough. I'd forgotten they'd be here, actually. Chris told me the kids would have the house to themselves tonight, but it seems their parents have invited their friends, too. Oh, well – another Greek experience for you. Swim?"

They stripped off their clothes to their bathing suits, then plunged into the pool, laughing at the shock of the cold water. After they'd splashed round for a while, Rachel gave Stavros an appraising look. He really was a stunning guy – strong, muscular, with those dark, intense good looks and a quick intelligence that lit up his velvety eyes.

"So what's your secret?" Rachel asked lightly.

"What do you mean?" he asked. "Are you talking about my champion backstroke? My amazing ability to select good parties to show off to my English friends? Or my skill at doing this?" And he flipped right over in the water, snaked through Rachel's legs, and somersaulted up again to the surface.

She laughed. "No, actually I was wondering about your love life," she said.

Stavros looked offended. "What do you mean?"

"Oh, don't be so stuffy, Stavros," Rachel teased, remembering how Alison was convinced that Stavros must have a secret love affair. "We're all on to you, you know."

"What do you mean?" asked Stavros in alarm.

Rachel eyed him curiously, wondering whether her teasing had struck a nerve. "Oh, we just thought you must have a girlfriend hidden away somewhere. You never flirt with the clients — not even as much as Alex does, and he's actually going out with someone."

"Yes, well, if I was going out with her I would not behave as he does," Stavros snapped. "I do not believe in this flirting — to me, it is just playing with people. It is not honourable. Someone could get hurt."

"That's exactly what I mean," Rachel said. "You are being faithful to someone, aren't you? And you should be able to tell us. We're your friends."

"Yes, you are a good friend, Rachel," Stavros answered stiffly. "And as a good friend, you will not ask me these personal questions. A good friend knows when to interfere — and when to keep quiet."

With that, he swung up the ladder at the side of the pool and disappeared. Rachel looked after him, feeling rather foolish. Then she shrugged. If he wanted to be so private it was up to him. But she couldn't help feeling he must have something to hide. Thoughtfully, she pulled herself out of the water, dried herself with one of the towels draped nearby, and put her skirt back on over her bathing suit, hoping it would dry quickly.

As she made her way back up the garden a familiar voice hailed her. "Hello, darlin'! Well I never! Fancy seeing you here."

Gerald was standing with a group of very smart Greek men in evening suits. He himself was wearing a white tuxedo with sequins bordering the lapels. He looked a little like a clown, but there was something almost distinguished about him, too, Rachel thought. He certainly had a genius for turning up in unexpected places.

Now he beckoned her over and took her arm. "This is the one I've been telling you about," he said to a man at his side. "This is Rachel Stanley. Works for Dream Ticket but I'm always telling her she's made for better things. Rachel, meet my mate Socrates Kolynos."

The man gave her an elaborate bow. "How do you do," he said in impeccable English. "I have heard a great deal about you."

"Good, I hope," Rachel answered shyly.

"Oh – very, very good, very interesting," he assured her. "I always like to hear about young ambitious people. The world does not have enough of them, I think."

"So, er, what do you do?" Rachel asked politely.

"Come on, now, Rachel – Socrates Kolynos! You must have heard of his company," Gerald broke in. "You deal with them all the time."

Rachel frowned. "Kolynos," she said, then shook her head. "No, sorry, I don't think so."

"Not Kolynos, brainhead," Gerald scoffed. "Socrates! His company's called Socrates. Now, does that mean something to you?"

"Oh, the shipping company," Rachel breathed, impressed. "Yes, indeed – we do a little business with you here in Ephros. We use your boats for our day trips quite a lot."

Socrates bowed again. "That is a small diversion

for us," he explained. "My son, Tony, he runs the local tourist operation. He likes to have something entirely his own. At first, I tell him not to waste his time. There are bigger, more important things he could be doing. But he insisted, he worked hard, he built the operation himself. Now it is doing very well, very well. In fact, we are thinking of expanding. So, I am very proud of my son. There he is — over there."

He pointed to a slim, athletic-looking guy who was talking earnestly to the girl at his side. Rachel glanced at them, looked away, then glanced back again with a jolt. The girl by his side, nodding so animatedly, her eyes wide and adoring, was Alison. The two of them floated past, clearly aware of nothing and nobody but each other.

"I knew I had seen you before somewhere," Tony was saying to Alison. "You came to that party the other night with Stavros, yes?"

Alison nodded. "That's right. I remember you, too. You were telling me about deep-sea diving and all the creatures you get to see underwater."

Tony blushed. "Yes, that was probably me. I always talk about fish when I really fancy a girl. I don't know why. I wish I didn't. It's nerves, or something. No wonder you went off and danced with someone else."

"Oh, I didn't mean to," Alison assured him earnestly. "I thought you were fascinating. But the music was so loud, and everyone was dancing and—"

"I know!" Tony said forcefully. "And you waited

for me to ask you and when I didn't you thought I wasn't interested. I could kick myself!" And he beat his fist hard against his forehead a few times, until Alison, laughing, begged him to stop.

She was surprised at herself. So far, this summer, she'd enjoyed meeting lots of boys and flirting with all of them. Tony had been no different – just another lovely-looking Greek boy. But now, meeting him again, she was beginning to feel differently about him. He was so very sweet. And clearly so interested in her.

"Look, I was shy," he said gently. "Then, I thought maybe you were with Stavros. I don't know him very well, you see."

"No, I work with Stavros but I'm certainly not with him," Alison assured him. "In fact, no one ever is. That's one of the mysteries about Stavros. He could get any girl he wants, but he never seems to be with anyone."

"That is good – and bad," Tony said meaningfully. "Good – that you are not his girlfriend. Bad – that he can get any girl he wants. Because that means you would be his girlfriend – if he asked."

Alison vigorously shook her head, her wild curls bobbing up and down. "No – no, of course not. I didn't mean that at all."

"Good," Tony murmured. "That is good. Now, perhaps, you would like to dance with me?" He led her to another part of the house where a disco had been set up. The room was full of young people dancing to a loud, booming rhythm as the lights flickered and winked all round them.

As Tony and Alison stepped on to the floor the

music quietened down to a slow, dreamy classic –
"I Will Always Love You". Tony took her in his
arms and they began to dance, swaying gently
together as the powerful, wailing vocal rose to a
crescendo of passionate emotion.

As the song ended, Tony didn't release his grip,
merely held on to her tighter. The next number
was another slow, tender love song. As they
drifted round the floor, their bodies moving
together in an almost mystical unison, Alison
began to think she must be in a dream. Tony was
having such a strange and powerful effect on her.
She'd never met anyone remotely like him. Yet, at
the same time, she had this curious feeling that
somehow, inexplicably, she'd known him all her
life.

"It is so strange," he murmured, his lips caressing her hair. "I hardly know you. Yet the minute
I saw you I knew you were someone special. As
though we'd known each other for ever and you
were just waiting for me to come and find you."

Then, as the music lingered on, his lips found
hers, and they were locked together in their first,
sweet kiss – a kiss that Alison wanted to last for
ever and ever.

10

Late on Saturday afternoon Jack sat at his
desk, staring darkly at the photograph in
front of him. He and Mariella had dealt with the
morning mail when she handed him an envelope
postmarked Ephros. The address had been typed
by computer on to a label. But scrawled in capitals
in the top corner were the words: "Personal.
Confident. Private."

The picture was of Rachel, smiling into the
camera. A man with thinning hair and a shiny
face had his arm round her and was looking at her
fondly. There was a feeling of intimacy about the
pose – something that made Jack feel uncomfortable and miserable and angry all at the same
time.

Before he'd had a chance to recover from the
shock of seeing the photograph there was a knock
on his door and Mariella was ushering in a suave,
immaculately dressed, middle-aged Greek man.
Jack stood up to welcome him. Socrates Kolynos

had made the appointment to visit him a couple of days before. And from what Jack had heard, this was not an offer you could turn down.

Socrates Kolynos had made his millions through a very complicated and high-powered shipping business. But these days he had interests in all kinds of offshoots. Including tourism.

"Sit down, sit down, my good man," he said suavely, pumping Jack's hand up and down. "I am delighted to meet you, really. My old friend Theodore has told me how well you are running this operation here for Dream Ticket. This is something I like very much to see – hard work and effort in young people. You know, I have endowed a new college here in Athens, a special college devoted to tourism and travel. I have made sure there are many scholarships for deserving youngsters. Further education here in Greece is expensive, yes? But education is the way out of poverty. I should know."

He launched into a long story about how he came from a poor family, a family with no prospects. And how if he could make it, that showed that it could be done. And that was why he was so keen to stay in contact with young people and to try and help them to achieve what he had achieved. Jack was impressed, but all the time was wondering what he wanted, what was the real purpose of this visit.

"My son, Tony," Socrates went on. "Now he is a good boy, a very good boy, but sometimes I wonder – does he have it too easy? He knows where his next meal is coming from, always. He never goes without. He does not know the meaning of struggle. And yet –" he smiled modestly – "I hope I have taught him well. He is running a good business himself now, you know, supplying boats for tours and trips. Very nice. I watch him and I think, yes, maybe we should be investing more time in this travel, you know? So, what do you think?"

Jack looked baffled. "What do I think about what?"

Socrates laughed heartily. "You funny man, very funny. You don't know? I am asking your advice on a business matter. I have heard that my old friend Theo may be thinking of selling his company, yes? I have been hearing this, talking with old friends, contacts. There is a lot of interest, I think. There are those who need to know a little more about the Greek operation, yes? People ask, I agree to find out."

Jack was alarmed. He must surely mean he was thinking of buying the company himself. "I'm afraid there's very little I can tell you, Mr Kolynos," he said formally. "I suggest you speak directly to Theodore if you wish to discuss the business of Dream Ticket. My files here are strictly confidential, I'm afraid, and it would be most improper for me to reveal any part of our dealings to anyone."

Socrates was not the least put off. "Well said," he remarked. "Theo was right, you are a good manager, very good, very loyal. This makes me even more sure that Dream Ticket is indeed a company worth considering. I met another

105

excellent young person just the other day. A fine young woman, a holiday representative. Her name, let me see, her name was Rachel something."

Jack's heart jumped. "Rachel Stanley?" he asked sharply.

Socrates smiled and thumped the table with his fist. "That's the one. Rachel Stanley. Very good, very tough girl. I have heard much about her through my ... er, my ... contacts. I think you better do a little thinking, young man. In case there are, how shall we say – in case there are changes coming, yes? Your colleague Rachel, you know, I have a feeling that she will not be with you for too much longer. My sources inform me that Rachel is considering a move very, very seriously."

He got up soon afterwards, still radiating benevolence and goodwill. He shook Jack heartily by the hand once again. "Good to meet you, very good," he said. "This is a tip for you, for the future. No matter how successful you become, no matter how rich and powerful, you must always stay on the ground. Do not rely on others to tell you what is going on or your instincts will run dry. This is why I make my visits. This is how I keep fresh. Goodbye, and good luck. I will see you again."

This was not a polite hope, Jack realized as the door shut behind his visitor. This was more of a threat! His head was whirling with confusion and shock. First there was that picture of Rachel. Then Socrates hinted that she was thinking of leaving the company. Then his announcement of his intention to buy up Dream Ticket. Jack wondered why he had bothered to come in person to see him. Maybe he was in Athens anyway, he decided. He liked to stay in touch with what was going on, he'd said so himself. But the more Jack thought about it, the more he began to think that Socrates had not paid that visit to find out anything at all. He'd come to warn him. Or, maybe, to threaten him...

Mariella appeared in the doorway, a pleading look on her face. "Jack, it's five o'clock."

"Oh, I'm sorry," Jack said at once. "It's terribly late. Of course, you must go home. I should have said so before."

"I don't want to," Mariella said, pouting. "I'd rather be with you. Listen, I've been here in Athens for three weeks now and all I've done is work, work, work. And you've been even worse. I know how late you stay, trying to sort out the chaos here. It's time we both had a break and saw some of the sights. Come on, Jack — you really look like you need to relax."

A few hours later, after they had wandered through little market streets and busy shopping precincts, after they had eaten kebabs at a little outdoor restaurant, and tasted yoghurt and honey from a street barrow, Jack and Mariella were climbing the steep, rugged hill of the Acropolis, Athens' most famous sight. It was a long, strenuous haul. All the way up, Jack was trying to sort out the muddled thoughts that crowded into his brain. Socrates wanted to buy Dream Ticket — but he cared about young people. Maybe that was

107

why he'd decided to warn Jack about the possible buy-out. On the other hand, businessmen of his calibre were not usually famed for their acts of kindness. It was more likely that he'd come to threaten him. Telling him that Rachel was thinking of leaving could just have been a way of making him panic.

Socrates couldn't know that Rachel leaving Dream Ticket would be tantamount to Rachel leaving him, too. Unless Socrates knew that they were together... Who were his so-called contacts, in any case? His mind flashed then to that picture – that balding man with the satisfied grin, smiling at Rachel possessively. Was he a boyfriend? If not, why was he looking at her like that?

Jealous, angry and bewildered, Jack carried on climbing the hill, glad of the exertion which helped to relieve some of the anger and stress that was eating away at him. Then, about half-way up, he stopped as a plaintive voice called from behind him.

"Jack?" Mariella was floundering along a few metres behind him. "Give us a hand, would you?" she asked, panting. "I'm not used to climbing."

Briefly, Jack thought of Rachel – the time she had climbed down a clifftop, dangling from a rope, to rescue an injured girl ... he thought of Rachel swimming, those long, powerful strokes as she ploughed effortlessly through the water ... then, painfully, he remembered the feeling of Rachel in his arms, her slim frame cleaving passionately to his...

He shook his head, as if to shake out the images of Rachel. It hurt too much to think about her, about all their times together, and then to think of that picture, those hints of her betrayal. He clambered down to Mariella and grasped her outstretched hand. She felt soft. She was smiling gratefully at him, her eyelashes flickering invitingly. Jack realized he was glad to be holding her hand and then her elbow. He didn't want to let go.

By the time they reached the top of the hill it was dark. The gracious ruins, a tribute to a venerable and ancient civilization, towered over the vista, floodlit and splendid. Below them, the whole of Athens glittered. It was a hot, balmy evening. They were standing at the top of one of the most beautiful sights in the world.

Jack looked down at Mariella – her lovely face gazed up at him. Ruthlessly he banished the flickering images of Rachel which still tormented him. Instead, slowly and deliberately, he took Mariella in his arms. She felt pliant and willing as he pulled her towards him. Then she sighed with pleasure as their lips met.

It was with a heavy heart that Stavros made his way along the jetty to the glittering yacht. It was decked out with a spectacular display of lights and flags in honour of the big party. But they didn't seem welcoming to Stavros. It was more as if they were mocking him.

It had been difficult to get away from the others that evening. They hadn't planned anything special – just a simple meal in their favourite beach taverna. But to Stavros, struggling into his evening suit and slipping through the fire exit at the back of the Hotel Elena, it sounded perfect. Instead, he would be joining a crowd of fabulously rich people on a luxury yacht in the most ostentatiously wealthy marina in the whole of Greece. He'd be offered champagne and oysters, freshly-caught lobster dressed with a fine sauce, and dishes groaning with exotic spicy delicacies.

Stavros sighed as he stepped through the flimsy curtains into the bowels of the ship. He was thinking about the restaurant where the others would be laughing and joking, chucking olives into each other's mouths and mopping up salad dressing with huge hunks of sesame bread.

"Darling – at last!" A blonde woman, reeking with perfume, glittering with gold jewellery, tottered towards him on high, pointed gold sandals. She was heavily made-up over a dark tan that made her blonde tresses appear even more unlikely. She took Stavros' face with both her hands and gazed at him hungrily.

"I have missed you, my darling," she went on caressingly, in Greek, then pulled his face down to hers in a passionate, possessive kiss.

"Yes, me too," Stavros mumbled. "It's – it's good to see you, Helen. I'm sorry it's been so long. I've been working very hard…"

"I know, I know." She dismissed his excuses impatiently. "Always you tell me how hard you work. Melina and Ariadne, they saw you working very, very hard last week at a party, I hear."

"I managed to get away that night," Stavros admitted, following her into the throng. "I was hoping so much you might be there."

"Oh — I have been busy too, my pet. My agent, he sends me one script for a horror film. I play the stepmother. I say, no thanks. Then another script for a romantic comedy. I am the mother-in-law. I say, no thanks. He pleads. I plead. We talk, we quarrel. I say, why do you consider these parts for me? I am the most glamorous actress in Greece, yes?"

"Of course you are," Stavros assured her, his arm round her waist, his lips pressed against the hard shell of her dangling earrings. "You are a great star and you must be treated like one. Why not change your agent?"

She laughed derisively. "That is not so easy, you know? In this business you come across crooks, cheats, people who want your money. People with no — with no principles. No, I stay with the one I know. He is at least honest. But he must come up with a better part for me, that is all I ask."

"Maybe these parts he offers you are very big roles," suggested Stavros.

She shrugged. "Yes, he tells me they are. But no, my darling, Helen knows better. He is just trying to convince me to take something that will be good for him, for his reputation. Maybe he is saving other parts for his other clients. But none, none will ever bring him the fortune that I have. None will have the stature of Helen Sappho."

People were milling round the covered deck, screeching recognition, kissing on both cheeks, exclaiming and extolling. As Helen and Stavros mingled in the crowd she was repeatedly accosted by other middle-aged people in expensive clothes and sparkling jewels, all piling on flattering words and talking of deals and contracts, options and projects.

"All of this – this world, it is so false," Helen whispered to Stavros as they began to dance. "Since I met you, my darling, I have come to realize what I really want. You are so sweet, so honest, so unspoilt. You are good for me, Stavros. And I –" she went on, her eyes glittering – "I am good to you, no?"

Stavros sighed. There was no denying it. Helen was the kindest, the most generous of lovers. She showered gifts on him, she made few demands, she encouraged him in all that he wanted to do, without standing in his way. "All I ask in return," she would tell him, "is a little love. This is what I need from you."

Then came the moment he'd been dreading, and yet hating himself for dreading. "Come down to my cabin," she whispered in his ear. "I have something for you, yes?"

Without protest, Stavros followed her reluctantly away from the noisy, crowded party deck and down the steps to the living quarters. Every time he saw her there would be a similar ritual. A greeting. Then she would show him off to her friends. And then, the private moment when she would get him alone.

"I have a little gift for you," she told him coquettishly when they reached her cabin – a gold and pink boudoir festooned with cushions and soft, billowy drapes. She handed him a small, gold box. With trepidation, he opened it. There, nestling in a bed of black velvet, was a very expensive, state-of-the-art designer watch.

"Oh, Helen – no," stammered Stavros, overcome with guilt and a creeping sense of horror. "This is too much, too expensive. I can't accept it." He looked at her wretchedly. Her eyes had hardened to sharp, grit-like beads.

"What do you mean?" she demanded harshly. "You are too good suddenly to accept my gifts? Stavros, I have not seen you for two weeks, you say you are busy yet you have time to go to parties. You will not accept my gift of love and yet you seem happy to accept my help in other ways."

Stavros flinched. It was true – Helen was helping to pay his college fees. It was something she had offered to do generously and joyfully the previous year when they had met. Now, nine months later, it felt to Stavros more like a weapon than a gift – a dangerous weapon that gave her power over him and turned him into her slave, her prisoner. And he couldn't deny it, he thought unhappily. He was grateful to have a contribution to the expensive fees. More than anything he wanted to finish his university degree, complete his education. It hadn't seemed so very wrong to accept the help that had been offered so freely.

So now, loathing himself, he forced a smile to his lips. "Hush, Helen," he soothed her. "I only meant, I do not think you should squander your money like this. You are far too good to me. You give too much. When all I really want is you..."

He pulled her towards him and bent to kiss her. For what seemed a very long time this romance had felt more like a duty than a pleasure. He could barely remember those early, heady days when his affair with Helen had been an adventure of excitement and passion. Now, he felt nothing but a vague affection for this talented but fading movie star. Close-up, he could see the lines etching her face, the tell-tale wrinkles on her neck and her scarlet-fingered hands. So that now, as he pressed his lips to hers, he felt no spark of desire. Only tenderness and compassion.

But this time there was something else, too. As they kissed, as she arched towards him, trembling with longing, another face came into view, another body – lithe and strong and vigorous – haunted his mind. And the more they kissed, the more conscious he was of this other woman tormenting him, taunting him, beckoning him.

11

"Ladies and gentlemen, we shall shortly be approaching Ephros hot springs – one of the island's most intriguing natural resources," chanted Alison as the coach careered crazily round a steep, craggy mountain path. It was the following Tuesday and another Dream Ticket excursion was under way. "For centuries people have flocked here to sample the healing waters, to bathe in the nourishing mineral pools and to relax, soothed by the delicious hot jets."

"Hope they're more efficient than the plumbing in our hotel," muttered Tom Millington. "We could do with a hot jet or two in our shower, couldn't we, Enid?" His wife sneered her agreement, while those round them smiled nervously.

"I hope this trip is all it's cracked up to be," Lisa remarked, worried, to Alison. "All we need now is another disaster. Especially with the Millingtons on board."

"Don't worry, I've done my research," Alison

whispered back. "Tony told me all about the hot springs. Apparently people with terrible chronic illnesses swear they've been healed by the magic water of Ephros. And it's ever so pretty, too – with a fabulous view of the sea and the coastline. Oh, and there's a bar and souvenir shop, so there's something for everyone."

"Talking of Tony – how is he?" asked Lisa. "Still going strong?"

Alison grinned. "He's lovely," she said dreamily. "You'd never know that he comes from such a rich, powerful family. There's nothing snobby about him. If anything, he's very modest. And so sweet... So far we've just gone for a drink, or for a drive in the mountains. He says he wants to get to know me properly. But then – on Saturday night – he took me to this fabulous party."

"I thought you were going somewhere glamorous. You had that gorgeous black dress, and your hair was great, all pinned up like that," commented Lisa. "So – tell me!"

"It was on a yacht in Soliniki," Alison told her, her eyes shining at the memory. "It belongs to his father, really, but there are always loads of famous people visiting. Film stars, politicians, models – I felt as if I was in a movie myself, it was so luxurious. All I wanted to do was look at everyone, and dance. But Tony was quite bored. I suppose he's so used to the high life, he doesn't see it as anything special. And there weren't any people our age. Oh, except..." She tailed off thoughtfully.

"Except what? Or who?" demanded Lisa at once. "Go on, Alison, you're hiding something. I can tell."

Alison looked embarrassed. "It doesn't seem fair to say anything, really," she explained. "I mean — it's none of our business. And it might not even have been him."

Who?" persisted Lisa. "Who might it not have been, where?"

Alison sighed. "The main party was on the deck under a sort of decorated canopy," she explained. "It got very crowded and at one point Tony suggested that we go down to his cabin to cool off." She paused here and blushed. Lisa giggled.

"Anyway," Alison went on slowly, "I saw this couple. The door to their cabin was open and they were kissing..."

"Who?" Lisa almost screeched at her. "You're doing this on purpose!"

"Well, I could be wrong," Alison said. "I could easily be mistaken. But from where I was standing, I could have sworn it was Stavros. And he was kissing this woman really — um, well ... seriously."

"Wow!" was all Lisa could manage. She thought for a moment, then said slowly, "That would explain an awful lot, wouldn't it? No wonder he seems like such a loner if he's got a fancy girlfriend tucked away on a luxury yacht. What was she like? Was she gorgeous?"

Alison shook her head. "Definitely not. I'd say she was much older than him, not that gorgeous at all. But she had masses of jewellery and a really expensive dress."

"Maybe she was his mother," suggested Lisa.

"Not a chance," Alison said. "Not the way those

two were carrying on. I remember being a bit surprised, but I didn't have much time to think about it. I asked Tony if it was Stavros and he wasn't sure. He doesn't know him that well. In any case, he was interested in other things." Alison smiled her dreamy smile again.

"You're lucky," Lisa said wistfully. "If you two are so crazy about each other make sure you hang on to him. I think what you have together sounds very special."

"How about you and Alex?" Alison asked, curious. "You two seemed made for each other. But just lately you haven't been quite so happy, have you?"

Lisa shook her head sadly. "We're OK," she said. "We've sort of agreed that couples who've been together a long time do go through bad patches. But when I see two people such as you and Tony, I remember what we used to be like and it doesn't feel that way any more." She shrugged and forced a bright smile. "Still, I shouldn't complain, should I? Alex is great, I know that. We can't expect the magic to last for ever."

Alison didn't have a chance to reply. The coach was pulling into the car park next to the hot springs. Everyone clambered out and assembled at the entry point.

"Welcome, ladies and gentlemen," said a very fat, very bald man with a thick, black moustache. "Welcome to Ephros Hot Springs. I am in charge here, my name is Kostas, I hope you have a very good time here. Let it all hang out, yes?"

"What does he mean?" demanded Enid Millington suspiciously.

"Oh, he wants you to relax and enjoy yourselves," Alison assured her as they followed him into the cool, dark entrance to the springs. "Come along, you need to go into the changing rooms and then we'll meet at the hallway down here."

While everyone was changing, Lisa remarked brightly, "Oh, well, at least it makes a change from running the Seashell Club."

"I don't know," Alison replied, jerking her head towards the Millington mother and daughters. "I don't know if you'll find it all that different."

Once they'd gathered at the meeting point, Kostas led the party into what looked like a huge, tiled swimming pool. He gestured to them to get into the water. It was warm, with hot jets gushing from behind them. Just to add to the sensation, Kostas walked round behind each person, directing more jets on to their backs from a series of entwined pipes which fed from the walls.

"'Ere, do you mind?" exclaimed Tom Millington. "Keep your distance, will you?" But Kostas, who clearly knew very little English, just beamed and took no notice.

"You like?" he asked happily. Other people started to look nervous, and began to back away from him as he advanced with his jets of bubbling water. The more they cringed the more anxious he became to direct the water all over them.

Oblivious, Kostas announced happily, "Now, you have seen our first pool. It is time to move to our smaller, intimate pool, yes?"

People began to scramble out, relieved. "Who will go first?" he asked. The Millingtons – who had been the first out of the pool – were nearest to the door. "This way," he beckoned.

They followed him through a narrow tunnel to a much smaller room, with a pool about the size of a jacuzzi. There was room for only about eight people. Lisa and Alison joined the Millingtons and one other couple. Kostas frowned at them.

"No – for this pool you need no clothes," he said. "You understand? I show you!" To the horror of them all, he removed his own trunks. Enid covered her children's eyes. Tom bellowed; the other couple screamed.

"What on earth do you think you're doing!" Alison yelled at him. "Are you completely, totally out of your skull?"

"But I don't understand," Kostas said, genuinely bewildered as the angry group left the pool, muttering that they would call the police, a lawyer, the British consul. "Yesterday, a very nice English man he was here. He took the waters with me. I tell him – a party of English people are coming. He say, be sure to give them a special good time, Kostas. Be sure they take off all their clothes. They will expect it. They be disappointed if not..."

"He must have been joking with you," Alison told him angrily. "Now, I think we'd better just leave."

Swiftly, Lisa and Alison shepherded their bewildered party together, apologizing, cajoling, explaining, soothing. "Terrible mistake," they were saying. "Normally this is a wonderful outing – we'll go again next week."

"Not likely!" jeered Tom Millington. "You'll not

find us spending good money coming here again. I've a good mind to complain to the authorities."

"And you'd be quite right," Lisa assured him calmly. "Don't worry, that's just what we intend to do. Let's have a nice drink in a café on the way home, shall we? And if we leave now, we'll be in time for a nice swim back home."

As the threats and mutters began to die down, and the coach pulled away, she whispered to Alison, "You were right! They're ten times worse than the under-fives, this lot. And a lot more trouble!"

Alex had spent the afternoon helping Rachel at the Seashell Club. He'd quite enjoyed looking after the little children. They were so much less complicated than the grown-ups. Especially the grown-up girls.

As they were locking up the Club, a familiar, bronzed figure shimmered by. It was Astrid, with her friend Mary. "Alex! Hi!" she waved. "You are free now? How about coming for a swim with us? We have a nice lilo – there's lots of room."

Alex looked at Rachel, who just smiled. "You go ahead, Alex," she said. "It was really nice of you to help me on your free morning. You deserve a swim. I'll catch up with you later."

Soon Alex was splashing happily in the water with the two girls, trying to tip them off the lilo amid a great deal of screaming and laughter. Then someone produced a beach ball, and they played a wild game which involved everyone diving in turn off the lilo to try and catch the ball.

He was enjoying himself hugely. It seemed to have been a very long time since he'd had this kind of fun. He couldn't help feeling relieved that Lisa was away for the day. Somehow, it would have been more difficult to join in with the girls if she had been around. These days, he felt guilty an awful lot of the time, and he just wasn't sure why.

But there was no time to start analysing his feelings. He reached for the ball and chucked it right over Mary's head towards the shore. Astrid slid off the lilo, swam after the ball until she was in her depth, then gave a flying leap and caught it. And then she screamed – a sharp howl of surprise and pain.

Alex was by her side in an instant and helped her to dry land. She was limping heavily, her face white under the dark tan. "My foot," she said weakly. "Something has bitten me. Oh – I don't like to look!"

Alex wasn't too keen himself, but he took her foot in his hand and peered at it. A black, spiky sea urchin was embedded right in the ball of her toe. "Oh, bad luck," he said, trying to sound calmer than he felt. "It's a – well, never mind what it is. Hang on!" He wrapped his T-shirt round his hand and then grabbed hold of the creature and pulled hard. There was a sickening, crunching sound as he squeezed it hard in the bound palm of his hand.

"All out," he announced. Then he glanced at Astrid. Her face was still distorted with pain. "Look, I'll get you back to the hotel right now," he told her. "It's not far. I know there's something in the First Aid kit for that sting, and I'll need to make sure there's nothing left in your foot."

Between them, he and Mary managed to half carry Astrid back to the hotel. Alex took her to his own room, which was nearest, and sat her on the bed while he fetched the First Aid kit. Astrid must have told Mary she'd be OK, because when he returned, she was alone in his room.

Concentrating hard, he sprayed the antihistamine on to the swelling until it was frozen. "That should soothe the pain for a while," he said, trying to sound knowledgeable. "Now, let me get a good look at that foot." He took her foot gently in his hand and shone a torch at the wounded area. "No, I think you're OK," he said at last. "I can't see any more spikes there. You're lucky – it was a very nasty thing to happen." He put down the torch, but somehow he still held Astrid's foot, and found that he was gently, rhythmically stroking first the foot, then her ankle. He felt as if he was under some strange spell, and all he wanted to do was to carry on holding her and stroking her.

After a while, he looked up and saw that she was staring at him with an inviting, heavy-lidded gaze. Very, very slowly he edged towards her, closer and closer until he could feel her breath, light and soft against his neck. And then he was kissing her, her arms crept round him and she pulled him down towards her until he was lost in oblivion, and all he could think of was her lips, her taste, her nearness.

*   *   *

Lisa flung open the door, about to exclaim

excitedly about the disastrous events at the hot springs. Instead, she simply stood in the doorway open-mouthed. Alex, her Alex, was entwined in the arms of a blonde girl. She vaguely recognized her. They were kissing so hotly that as they sprang away from each other you could almost hear the tear. For a few moments all three of them were silent.

Then Lisa turned and rushed away, hot tears springing to her eyes. "Lisa – no, wait!" Alex called after her. But she didn't stop to listen to him, didn't wait to hear what he could possibly have to say to her.

Sobbing, she ran out of his room, down the corridor of their apartment block, out of the back door to the garden – where she plummeted head first into Stavros who was idly practising his basketball shots. "Hey! Slow down," he gasped, slightly winded from the impact. He took her by the shoulders for a moment, then realized she was crying.

"Lisa! It's OK, it's OK," he soothed her as if she was a little girl. Very gently, he held her against him, stroking her hair rhythmically until her sobs had died down.

Lisa nestled against him, grateful for the simple comfort he offered – grateful that he didn't ask what was the matter, or whether she was all right. He was a good friend, she thought fondly. A really good guy.

After a while, though, she found herself pouring out her heart to Stavros as they sat sipping lemonade by the pool. "You know, it's funny," she reflected, puzzled. "I think I should feel worse than this."

"I will never understand the English," grinned Stavros. "You feel bad because you don't feel worse?"

Lisa laughed tremulously. "Silly! I just meant that I don't feel completely gutted, or useless, or badly hurt, not really."

"Well, you don't exactly look like you've won the lottery," Stavros said, staring at her in concern.

"No," agreed Lisa. "But it's not hurt I feel. It's two parts anger to one part sadness. Anger that Alex could betray me – in his own room, where I've been with him so often. And sadness – that things have gone so wrong between us that he'd want to."

For some reason Stavros seemed vastly amused by this. "Two parts anger to one part sadness," he repeated. "This is a very good formula for broken hearts. I think I'll suggest that Michael puts it on the cocktail menu. We should offer it as a special drink for lovers."

"Ex-lovers," Lisa corrected him.

"I'll drink to that," joked Stavros. Then, solemnly, he clinked his plastic glass against hers and they drank a toast to anger, sadness and lovers everywhere.

12

As Jack strode along the long, dusty pathway to the hotel on Wednesday evening, a familiar figure came rushing out to greet him and flew headlong into his arms. "Jack! Oh, Jack – it really is you!" gasped Rachel happily. "I didn't believe you'd ever get here!"

He clasped her in a long, tight hug, his lips pressing against her hair. It felt so good to be with Rachel again – as if he'd come back home to where he belonged. As they walked arm in arm to the hotel, the sun sinking slowly into a bright yellow sky, he wanted so badly to believe that all his doubts about her had been mistaken. And yet – and yet...

"I was beginning to think you didn't really want to come," Rachel confided, hugging his arm happily as they made their way hip to hip along the dusky road. "All those excuses—"

"They weren't excuses," Jack put in quickly. "It's been crazy these last few weeks. I've never come across so many mix-ups all at once. There was one party of eight we'd booked into a hotel in Corfu when they wanted apartments in Crete. And one lot arrived in Kos a whole week early! The poor rep was actually crying down the pay phone for about ten minutes."

"So what did you do?" asked Rachel, trying to imagine how she would have coped.

"Oh, her money ran out in the end," Jack answered.

"Not about the rep crying," laughed Rachel. "About the Kos party, silly!"

Jack tapped his finger against his nose. "Contacts, my dear," he said in a funny voice. "I phoned a few mates, found a hotel which wasn't quite built and persuaded a few people it was ready for business."

Rachel gasped. "But what about the safety? Fire regulations? How did you do it?"

"I took care of all that," Jack reassured her airily. "Don't get so uptight, Rachel. It was all fine. I was just telling you to show you how busy I've been."

"And there I was thinking you must be having this great time living it up in Athens," Rachel teased.

Jack felt a pang of guilt as he recalled that evening with Mariella – the softness of her hand in his, the invitation in her eyes, the feel of her lips when he kissed her. Nothing had happened between them since then, but Mariella had made it quite clear that she was available, and that she wanted him. Was it possible to want two women?

he wondered, troubled. What was happening to him?

Now they'd reached the hotel and Rachel was unlocking her door. As soon as they were inside she turned to him. "Alone at last," she sighed, then stepped towards him, her arms twining round his neck. As their lips met the familiar rush of longing surged through him.

"Rachel, I've missed you so much," he groaned, his hands sliding down her taut, wiry body. There was something strong and wild about Rachel – a streak of independence that never failed to intrigue him. He remembered Mariella, her eyes wide and helpless as she struggled up the hill, begging for help. Rachel would never have done that, he thought affectionately. She would have prided herself on getting to the top first – then maybe offered him a helping hand.

Now, she was guiding him gently to the bed, pulling him down to her, her body arched towards his, her face flung back in surrender. For a moment, Jack gazed at her face beneath him – the face that he'd seen laughing with a stranger on that snapshot. Was it possible that this girl, his own beautiful girl, could be betraying him?

"I love you, Jack," she whispered. "I want you so much..." And then he was lost. Mariella, the man in the picture, the fear that Rachel might be leaving – all the complicated worries that had tormented him were banished. His whole being was on fire for Rachel and nothing else mattered – nothing else existed...

* * *

"OK, everyone, I'm sure you've enjoyed your lunch," announced Lisa above the excited shouts of the children and the general hubbub and chatter in the busy restaurant. "Now you have a whole afternoon on this lovely island. There's a market to explore and some lovely shops if you fancy getting some unusual souvenirs. Or you can just enjoy this beautiful beach which is said to be one of the finest in this region. That way, to your right, is the more populated area with a whole range of water sports for the more adventurous. Down there, if you walk for a mile or so, there's a lovely secluded inlet where you might catch a glimpse of some unusual wildlife. There are meant to be baby turtles there…"

Lisa rattled on, a confident beam fixed to her face. So far, she thought, they'd been lucky. The boat trip to the island had been smooth and pleasant. Everyone had clustered on deck to enjoy the view of the little islands all round them. Even lunch had been a success, with just the right blend of familiar food and unusual delicacies.

With satisfaction, Lisa noted that the Millingtons, for once, seemed to be unable to find anything to complain about. "If they look miserable we must be doing something right," she confided to Stavros. "They're only really happy if there's a nice juicy crisis to spoil the day."

"They should find that pretty difficult here," agreed Stavros. "Tykonos is a lovely island – it's one of my favourites. I will show you."

"Great," answered Lisa. She turned back to the party of some forty people, all jostling now to leave the restaurant. "Enjoy your day," she told them, still beaming. "And don't forget, we meet back here at five-thirty. The boat will be leaving at six o'clock. And I'd hate to leave any of you behind."

She turned to Stavros. "So – where are you taking me?"

Without replying, Stavros led her down to the vast, sandy beach, and they began to walk along the water's edge. They wandered amicably past families splashing in the waves, young couples playing jokari, children attempting to play football with a beachball... Soon they'd left the crowds behind them and walked on, passing the occasional outcrop of rock and cactus.

Lisa hadn't felt so relaxed for weeks. There had been so much tension between her and Alex that she'd begun to feel on edge whenever they were together. And then, just two days ago, there had been that spectacular scene when she'd found him on the bed with Astrid. He'd apologized, of course – claimed he'd got carried away. But that hadn't been enough to repair the rift between them. Now they were living out an uneasy truce, behaving politely enough when they were together, but preferring to avoid each other as much as they could.

"Let's give ourselves a cooling-off period," Alex had suggested. "Maybe that's what we need – so that when the time is right, we can maybe get back together."

Lisa had nodded agreement, secretly relieved that for a while she wouldn't have to worry about what Alex was thinking, what he was doing, what he was feeling.

Watching Stavros striding on ahead, Lisa felt grateful to him for letting her stroll along at her own pace. It made a change, being with someone who didn't expect anything of you, didn't criticize or take offence at what you did. She thought of Alex – who could be so sweet and considerate, but at other times was demanding, always knowing how to goad her and make her feel small.

After a while, they were alone on a stretch of barren, deserted wasteland, the water lapping against rough shingle and dust. Lisa was feeling very hot and tired. "Where are we going?" she whined. "This is horrible! Why couldn't we just stay on the beach where it was nice? We're miles away from the sun-loungers."

"Trust me," answered Stavros without even turning round. She sighed, and followed him.

After what seemed like hours, he stopped and waited for her to catch up. "Now," he said. "We are nearly there. Just round this corner."

"That's what they all say," complained Lisa. But she followed anyway. And when they'd rounded the corner she gasped. Before them, where the coastline undulated to form a little inlet, was a perfect, secluded beach, shaded by a cluster of palm trees and gently sloping cliffs.

Stavros sat down on a flat rock beneath a tree. "Thirsty?" he asked, and produced a flask from his rucksack. Lisa took a long gulp. It was just plain iced water, but it tasted more delicious than the most exotic wine.

He scrabbled deeper into the rucksack and emerged triumphantly with two snorkels, complete with masks. "This is a very good place for diving," he explained. "You can see lots of fish. You want to try?"

The next couple of hours were among the most magical Lisa had ever known. Stavros introduced her to a new, silent, enchanted world under the sea. Lisa soon got the hang of breathing through the snorkel and opening her eyes under the water. She was amazed and charmed by the seething life she encountered – shoals of tiny silvery fish, crabs peeping from under rocks, delicate fronds of seaweed feathering out from mottled stones and rocks.

Stavros was a very powerful swimmer and urged Lisa to more and more daring exploits. At one point he gestured towards a crop of rocks, a little way out to sea. "I'll race you there," he said, and set off without waiting for a reply.

Lisa was very strong and athletic but she was no match for Stavros. He reached the rocks long before she did, and sat casually sunbathing as she thrashed through the water to join him. The rocks were far further than they'd looked and Lisa was exhausted when she finally made it to the edge. She was hoping that Stavros would offer her a hand up but it obviously hadn't occurred to him that she might need help. He just lay in the sun, eyes closed, while she struggled up by herself.

"Oh, you made it then," he commented lazily when she reached his side. They lay companionably in the sun for a while until they agreed it was time to head back. Lisa immediately stood up and made a perfect dive off the rock. She was a graceful diver and wanted to show off to Stavros, to pay him back for being so much faster than her. At once, she wished she hadn't. As soon as she broke into the deep water she found herself caught up in a tangle of clammy, tenacious weeds.

The more she struggled to be free of them, the tighter their tentacles seemed to bind round her. At first she fought and tried to rip at the clingy strands. But, with rising panic, she realized she was being bound — trapped under the water, getting weaker and more breathless by the second. In fright, she opened her mouth to scream and it filled with water.

For a few moments she was suspended in sheer terror. Then two strong arms clasped her, as if from nowhere, and she was dragged away from the vicious plants and up to safety. Somehow, she was back on the rocks, coughing and spluttering. Stavros held her as she vomited out the bitter salt water.

"You OK?" he asked, when she was quiet. She nodded. "Not a good place to dive," he commented mildly.

"Well, how was I supposed to know that?" Lisa demanded. "You didn't tell me."

"You didn't ask," he answered. He seemed suddenly to realize that he was still holding her in his arms. Embarrassed, he jerked away from her. "Oh, well — no harm done," he said briskly. "Shall we go back?"

Furiously, Lisa struggled after him, back to the pretty little cove. He'd just saved her life. He'd held her tenderly while she was throwing up. And now he was treating her as though nothing much had happened.

"I did nearly die out there, you know," she complained as she staggered back on to dry land. "You could show a bit more concern."

"You don't need it," Stavros answered shrewdly. "You would be annoyed with a man who fussed over you."

Lisa knew this was true. "I wouldn't mind a bit of fuss," she protested.

"Well, that would be spoiling you, wouldn't it?" Stavros replied. He turned away from her and added quietly, "And I'm not the one who should be doing that."

That Thursday, long after Lisa and Stavros had taken the early boat to Tykonos, Rachel and Jack sat by the pool at the Hotel Elena, sipping coffee in the hot sunshine.

"It's funny how delicious coffee tastes here," Rachel mused. "You'd think it would be far too hot to enjoy a hot drink, but it just makes it better." She glanced tenderly at Jack. "Or maybe it's you that adds the extra flavour."

Jack smiled as she squeezed his hand, and quipped, "You make me sound like a tomato — grown for flavour."

"I'd say you were more of an orange," Rachel replied lightly.

"You mean, juicy and tangy and full of

goodness?" he asked.

"No — best when crushed," she answered. But even though she was smiling and joking, Rachel was feeling troubled. She couldn't quite understand why. It was so wonderful to be with Jack again. They'd had a perfect, passionate night. Everything should have been great. But somehow she could sense there was something wrong. And she didn't know what it was.

"I've missed you," she told him shyly. "It's been kind of lonely without you."

"Has it?" he said quite sharply. "Lonely, eh? I didn't realize that. So what exactly have you been doing to pass the time? Or should I say, who have you been doing it with?"

Rachel was astonished. There was a real coldness in Jack's voice, but she didn't understand what he was getting at.

"What — what do you mean?" she asked. "What are you getting at, Jack?"

"Nothing — forget it," Jack mumbled. "But if there's anything you want to tell me—"

"I don't understand," Rachel persisted. "What could I possibly have to hide?"

"Nothing. Never mind," Jack said quietly, shaking his head. "Look — I'm sorry, Rachel. I — I guess it's just a strain being away from you so much. Imagining you without me. Maybe I'm jealous..."

So Jack smiled, took Rachel's hand, changed the subject, and put his doubts right out of his mind. He'd thought about producing the photograph that was burning a hole in his pocket. He'd made

135

up his mind to ask Rachel outright about the man she was with — and about whether she was planning to leave Dream Ticket. But, somehow, he couldn't — he just didn't dare. And that was his big mistake.

Genuinely hurt and puzzled, searching her mind for what Jack might be referring to, Rachel thought about all the time she'd spent with Gerald — dear, funny, ungainly, vulgar, greedy, kind, friendly Gerald. No one could be jealous of him, she told herself — least of all Jack. On the other hand, she'd been vaguely relieved to find that Gerald was away for the weekend. It would have been complicated, explaining him to Jack — even though their relationship was so completely innocent. She decided it was best not to mention him at all. And that, she reflected afterwards, was her big mistake.

"So where exactly is this famous boat of yours then?" demanded Tom Millington. There was a touch of jubilation in his voice. There was nothing he liked more than a disaster, Lisa reflected, annoyed.

It was six o'clock. Everyone had returned promptly to the harbour just as she'd asked. They'd all had a wonderful afternoon and were chattering excitedly, swapping stories and showing off souvenirs. Some of the children were playing on the beach nearby. Others were queuing for ice-creams. Everything had gone so smoothly. Until now.

"I'm sure it'll be along in a minute," she soothed.

"Let's hope you're right," he sneered disbelievingly.

Stavros beckoned Lisa away from the crowd. "I do not like this," he said, frowning. "Socrates — they are a very reliable firm. My friend, Tony, he runs the whole operation and I know them well."

"We always use them — they're the best," Lisa agreed. "That's why I know they won't let us down."

"And that's what worries me. We know they are always punctual, so what's going on?" demanded Stavros. "That boat should have been waiting in harbour at five-thirty. We were due to leave at six. I don't like this."

As if to echo his fears, a loud squalling broke out. Some of the children were fighting. A baby began to bawl. An impatient mother began shouting at her whining offspring. The mood of the crowd was becoming distinctly restless.

Uneasily, Lisa gazed at him, wide-eyed. "So — so what do you think we should do?"

"I'll phone," Stavros said, making up his mind. "While I find out what's happened to the boat I think you need to distract everyone. How about a ticket inspection? They always take up time. Say you need to collect the tickets now."

So Lisa set about creating the most complicated system possible for examining everyone's tickets, quite unnecessarily, pretending that she would have to keep them all until the boat was safely moored back at Ephros.

Just as she was depositing all the tickets in a large, official-looking envelope, Stavros reappeared.

137

She slipped over to where he hovered in the doorway of the ticket office. "Bad news," he said grimly. "The boat won't be here until nine."

"What?" shrieked Lisa.

"That's right. Someone changed the arrangement."

"So change it back!"

"I tried," Stavros told her. "But they have no more boats. Apparently they were definitely told the pick-up was nine o'clock."

"But who told them?" demanded Lisa, bewildered. "And how? I mean, this trip was fixed ages ago, along with all the other bookings with Socrates. We run a boat trip to Tykonos every two weeks. The times are always exactly the same."

"I know," nodded Stavros. "Except for this one. You know, it could be a mistake. But it is hard to see how. To me, it seems deliberate."

"You mean — someone is playing a joke on us?" asked Lisa, incredulous.

Stavros shrugged. "Maybe a joke. More likely, someone is trying to damage us. And I think whoever it is is succeeding." He gestured towards the now definitely mutinous party — where grumbling among the adults was even louder than the whining of the children.

"We've got to do something," urged Lisa. "And it'd better be good. We've got another three hours of this!"

"What do you suggest I do?" snapped Stavros. "Get into my Superman suit and fly them all home?"

"Doesn't have to be you!" retorted Lisa. "Wait

there!" She flounced away from him before he could stop her and disappeared into the busy seafront promenade, lined with shops and restaurants, crowded now with people returning from the beach and mingling with early evening shoppers.

A few minutes later she reappeared and marched back to the huddle of tourists, looking purposeful. Stavros followed, intrigued. Lisa clapped her hands to attract everyone's attention. "Listen, everyone," she began. "We have to announce a little change of plan, I'm afraid."

"Oh, yes," interjected Tom Millington. "We might have known. Come on, lass, spill the beans. What are you letting us in for now?"

"There has been a slight mix-up," Lisa admitted. "You see, you've only paid for the regular trip today. But as it happens, I now find you're booked for the de luxe version. Unfortunate, I know, but it means you'll have an extra three hours in Tykonos, a lovely night trip home with all the lights — and of course you'll be our guests for the super three-star special dinner. All for the regular price, as it's our mistake."

"You mean — we're getting the more expensive version at the cheaper price?" someone asked.

"That's right," Lisa nodded, the beam plastered to her face. "Lucky, aren't you?"

Enid Millington sniffed loudly. "I don't call it that lucky, being stuck here for three more hours. I was reckoning on being home before dark."

But other members of the party, convinced they'd struck a bargain, began to talk over her.

She tried once more. "Besides," she added. "I didn't notice a de luxe version on the brochure. I didn't even know there was such a thing."

"No, it's quite new," Lisa assured her rapidly. "We've tried it on just a few very select parties and it's been most popular. I'm quite sure you'll be delighted with the little luxury extras."

That did it. Everyone looked pleased and excited, and the Millingtons were forced to retreat into a sulky silence.

"You did that brilliantly," Stavros told her later, when everyone was seated in the pretty taverna overlooking the beach. Lisa had organized some impromptu games for the children while they waited for the food. Now everyone was tucking into a sumptuous feast and knocking back their free wine.

"I hope it'll be OK, though," Lisa said, worried. "I was lucky to find a restaurant that could accommodate such a big crowd at short notice. They're a bit pricey – but it was the only way to calm them down."

"Dream Ticket will cough up," Stavros assured her. "They're lucky to have you, you know. Now – while they're all happy, why don't we go and check out this boat?"

They wandered out into the warm dusky evening and made their way to the harbour. They leaned against the railing by a line of rocks, anxiously scanning the vast horizon, eerily lit by the fast-sinking sun. "There!" Lisa said excitedly, pointing out to sea.

Like an angel descending from heaven into the

desert, the little pleasure boat, framed by an arc of fairy lights, chugged towards them. It was nearly dark now. Behind them the street that ran along the harbour was bustling with market vendors, the restaurants and shops teeming with tourists.

Filled with relief that their crisis was over, Lisa turned to Stavros, smiling radiantly. "You were right," she told him. "This is a wonderful island. It suddenly seems like the most perfect place in the world."

Stavros gave her a long, appraising look. "Right now, I think it is," he said. Slowly, deliberately, he reached his hand to her chin, tilted her face up to his and kissed her. "I have wanted to do this for a very long time," he whispered.

Lisa gazed at him for a moment, startled, her lips burning from the contact with his. Stavros gazed back, his handsome face filled with longing, his dark eyes smouldering. And then she was in his trembling arms, her whole being melting in his rough, passionate embrace.

13

It was with a heavy heart that Stavros clambered along the gangway on to the yacht. Helen was waiting for him, as he knew she would be. She was reclining in a sun-lounger, showing off her ageing but still firm body in a bikini that seemed to be made entirely of gold chains. She wore matching gold sandals and gold coins dangled from her ears. By her side was a tall cocktail glass with a straw. From time to time she reached over languidly to take a sip, then returned to the important business of tanning.

But the moment she saw Stavros, Helen was suddenly alert and full of life. "Ah, my boy – he is come!" she shrilled, her face breaking into a smile. "Now there is some real sunshine in my life. And I have so much to tell you. Come—"

She got up and moved to a little table by the yacht's luxury pool, gesturing for him to come and sit beside her. "Champagne!" she ordered loudly, without consulting him. "And two glasses."

"Helen," began Stavros, not sure how he was going to continue. But he wasn't given a chance.

"Yes, I know, my love," she gushed. "So much to say. It is always this way. I am here waiting, waiting on this lovely, beautiful boat which has everything you need for the perfect holiday. And it is so..." She dropped her voice dramatically. "So — boring! Without you, all is boring. So, now you are here, I am happy. I have news — very good news. I have a part. It is very good, a film I like very much. It means I must spend some time in America. We start shooting in LA in two weeks."

His heart leapt. This was like a gift from the skies. If Helen was leaving Greece, maybe he would never need to say what he had planned.

"Of course, you must come and visit," she carried on happily. "Before you go back to university you will fly out and see me. In Santa Monica. It is so beautiful. A place for lovers..."

Stavros stared into his glass of champagne. The fizzing bubbles seemed to be mocking him. It would be so easy to keep Helen happy, to string her along, make her think everything was OK. That way, she'd carry on paying his tuition fees, at least for a while. Then, with any luck, the whole affair might just fade away.

But then he remembered that electric kiss just a few nights ago — the feel of Lisa's young, slender body in his arms, her open, honest eyes gazing into his. He'd been avoiding Lisa since then, unsure how to act with her. What would she say if she knew about Helen — a woman he didn't love, didn't even like sometimes? What would Lisa think if she knew he was only continuing the affair because Helen was paying for his education?

It didn't take much to work out the answer. Lisa would be disgusted. He wouldn't stand a chance with her, as long as he was embroiled with Helen. So, plucking up all his courage, he drew a deep breath.

"Helen, I have something to say, too," he began intently. "We need to talk."

There was a fraction of a second when the blazing morning sun seemed to fade into a chill. Her eyes narrowed. Then she composed her face once again.

"Oh, I do not like that phrase," she told him lightly. "I would much rather not talk, if it is all the same to you. Shall we swim? Would you like to come down to the cabin?"

"No!" Stavros rasped, too quickly. Her face registered the hurt, then returned to its usual composure. She looked at him steadily, waiting for him to go on.

"I'm very pleased for you," he began carefully. "It is great that you have a part you like. Wonderful that you will be filming in California. But I won't be visiting you there." He stopped for a moment; she continued to fix her eyes on him.

"It's over, Helen," he sighed. "I – I've met someone else..." The image of Lisa flashed before his eyes, filling him with strength.

But to his surprise, Helen seemed to change before his very eyes. She stood up to her full height and reached for a dazzling green and turquoise silk sarong which she draped gracefully over her shoulder. She looked magnificent, transformed utterly from the clinging, slightly vulgar creature she had been just minutes before.

"I see," she said quietly. "I see I have been a foolish woman."

"Helen, please—" Stavros interrupted. But she silenced him with a majestic wave of the hand.

"No, do not speak," she went on. "Do not tell me any more. It is enough. I have enjoyed our time together very much, but do not take me to be even more foolish than I am. I have always known it would have to end. You cannot dictate your feelings. When love descends, all is lost."

Stavros gaped at her in awe and admiration. It was as though she was speaking someone else's lines. And then, with sudden insight, he realized that was exactly what she was doing. Helen had decided to play a role. She wasn't the possessive, voluptuous mistress any longer, but an older, wiser, gracious woman bowing out with dignity and retaining her pride. You had to hand it to her, Stavros thought. She was good – very good.

"I wish you well, Stavros," she was saying now, in carefully measured tones. "I think it best you go now, yes?" He nodded gratefully, wishing he was anywhere but here but at the same time aware that never had Helen appeared more beautiful or more impressive. "By the way," she added casually. "You needn't worry about next term. It is already paid. After that…" She smiled a little sadly. "Well, after that, you're on your own."

Stavros was speechless with gratitude and, he had to admit, with shame. Helen might be acting a new role, but there was nothing artificial about her generosity. "Helen — I've enjoyed it, too. I'll write — keep in touch," he stammered.

She shook her head. "No, you will not. Just good friends — only mad people believe in that. And English people. It is not for us. Go now, and I never want to see you again."

Stavros departed thankfully, but once he was on dry land again he realized, annoyed, that some of his clothes were still in Helen's cabin — left over from previous, happier visits. He'd better go back now, he decided, or it would be too late.

He made his way back to the deck but there was no sign of Helen. She must have gone down to the cabin. He followed, but stopped outside her door. There was a faint sound coming from inside. The door was slightly open so he peered round. On the bed was Helen, face down, collapsed and crumpled — and sobbing heart-rendingly into her pillow. This, then, thought Stavros, was what happened when the cameras stopped shooting. And all this pain had been caused by him.

Softly, he crept away, and left the ship. He was filled with remorse and self-disgust. He couldn't bear to think he had inflicted such torture. And if it could happen with one woman, who was to say it couldn't happen again. It was no good, he told himself. It just wasn't worth getting involved with anyone. It wasn't worth risking all that agony - all that guilt.

* * *

*"Oh, you'll never get to Heaven
In powder and paint
'Cos the Lord don't like
You as you ain't!"*

Everyone joined in the raucous chorus, as Rachel manoeuvred the jeep round another dangerous bend in the parched, rugged landscape. She thought she was probably driving a bit too fast but she was anxious to keep Lisa in view – and Lisa, who adored driving, was racing along, the dust flying in all directions behind her.

They were into the third fortnight of the summer now. The troublesome Millingtons had packed off back home, still muttering about disgraceful delays at airports and the terrible cost of souvenirs. Astrid's party had left, too, though now Lisa was rather wishing they were still here. It would have been simpler to deal with Alex.

The new party seemed to consist of quite a few families with teenage kids – too old to use the Seashell Club. Rachel had had the idea that they should lay on some special activities for the youngsters.

"Who better than us?" she'd pointed out to Lisa, and they'd both laughed, remembering the previous summer in Spain when they'd been in charge of the Hot Club.

"This lot look quite tame compared with last year," agreed Lisa. The Hot Club seemed to specialize in very lively, excitable, boisterous teenagers determined to have a really unforgettable time.

"They always look like that to start with,"

147

Rachel said darkly. "Give them a few days…" So they'd arranged that Alex would organize some football, Lisa would offer a teenage version of her extra-special aqua-splash classes. And later that week there was to be a disco specially for the youngsters, at the Elena.

Today, Rachel and Lisa were taking a party of girls to a petrified forest on the other side of the island. They'd booked out a couple of jeeps and were driving five girls each. None of the boys had signed up for the trip, and the reps were rather relieved.

"What is a petrified forest, exactly?" demanded Marsha, one of the younger girls. "Did it get frightened by a giant?"

Rachel laughed. "Not exactly," she told her. "It's just a geographical phenomenon. Because of the crosswinds here and various climatic oddities, the trees have turned to stone. It took thousands and thousands of years – can't just happen overnight."

"Will there be a café there?" demanded her friend Beth.

"I expect so," said Rachel. "But that's not why we're going. This is culture, right? Makes a change from beaches and swimming."

"And boys," someone added. They all giggled.

"That boy Dan who's always diving into the pool and splashing us," said Nina, one of the older girls, thoughtfully. 'He could do with a bit of petrifying. Is it possible to speed up the process, do you think?"

It took far longer than they'd imagined to reach the forest, driving through what amounted to a rocky desert landscape, dry and dusty, dotted only with the occasional clump of hardy, brown bushes and the odd cactus. But it was worth it. They were greeted by a friendly ticket collector who seemed to be expecting them.

"Ah, yes – my friend Gerald told me that maybe some English girls, they would arrive today," he said. Rachel tried to bite back her annoyance. It was true, Gerald had recommended the forest as a terrific outing. But she was always irritated at how Gerald seemed to know everyone and everything. It was almost as though he had spies everywhere.

But she had to admit he was right about the forest. It was like a large quarry, with pathways down and also up into higher levels. Although, as ever, it was a scorching hot day, there was plenty of shade and lots of resting places. After a strenuous climb up into one of the higher plateaux, Lisa and Rachel flopped down on to a couple of inviting-looking rocks.

"Just like old times," Rachel smiled, looking down at the little groups of teenage girls clambering around beneath them.

"In some ways," Lisa agreed with a sigh.

"You mean, Alex?" Rachel probed.

Lisa nodded. "It's no good pretending that it's working," she said. "We've tried that. We've been trying it all summer. The trouble is, I still love him. Well – I like him. He's like a really close friend who's becoming a stranger. It's become impossible even to talk any more. He thinks I'm still mad at him because of Astrid. But it's not that at all. Astrid would never have happened if we were together properly, like we used to be. Anyway, she's gone now and it all seems like so long ago. Especially now..."

Immediately, Rachel moved her face very close to Lisa's. "Aha!" she said triumphantly. "I knew something was going on. What is it, Lisa? Come on, you can tell me ... I am your very best friend."

"Stop it!" said Lisa crossly. "I was going to tell you anyway. I just haven't had the chance until now. It's — it's Stavros!"

"Wow!" breathed Rachel. "Really? Has anything happened?"

"Yes — and no," Lisa answered. Briefly, she told her about their day together on Tykonos, ending with that spectacular kiss. "I can't explain how it felt," she said dreamily. "He's gorgeous, of course. And we'd gone through such a lot that day... I don't know, Rachel, it was wild and exciting, but so sweet, at the same time. It just felt right. And it made me realize I don't belong with Alex any more."

"So — what now?" Rachel asked. "Does Alex know? Are you going out with Stavros now, or was it just a spur of the moment thing?"

Lisa frowned, perplexed. "No, and I don't know," she answered briefly. "I haven't seen Stavros properly since then, except when we're working. Never alone. Who knows, maybe he's avoiding me. Alex certainly is. Oh, Rachel — why does everything have to be so complicated?"

Rachel grinned. "It'll work out, Lisa," she comforted her. "You'll see. You and Alex will always be friends, I'm sure of it. And the sooner you get rid of all the bad feeling, the better. So even if nothing happens with Stavros, he's done you a favour, hasn't he?"

"Ye-es," replied Lisa thoughtfully. "But I want something to happen."

"Then it probably will," said Rachel. She smiled again at Lisa, glad that they were back on their old footing, friends against the world. "Come on, let's round up the kids and get going. It's a long journey back. I think we'd better see if we can stock up with drinks. It's going to be blistering, in the middle of the afternoon in that desert."

So, after a lot of calling, and waiting while the girls used the loos, and more waiting while they bought postcards and souvenirs and drinks, everyone piled back into the jeeps and began the hot, dusty trek back to Linoka.

For half an hour or so, Rachel concentrated on driving, thankful that the girls were too exhausted by the outing to chatter, let alone sing. Poor Lisa, she was thinking. It must be horrible, falling out of love. Briefly, she thought of Jack, and their weekend together. It had been as passionate as ever. She had felt just as in love. But all the same, she felt uneasy. Something had been wrong. Surely, she thought, surely Jack wasn't falling out of love with her?

At the very idea that she could lose him a sharp pain tightened round her heart. She remembered his sudden lapses into silence, almost as if he was angry with her, and his hints that he didn't trust her. Maybe, she thought fearfully, maybe it's Jack who isn't to be trusted. Could it be that Jack was seeing someone else and was trying to hint to her that she wasn't the only one in his life? But if that was the case, she told herself, then nothing made any sense, especially not Jack's jealousy.

But then all worries about Jack vanished. The jeep was making a very unhealthy sound, midway between a cough and a choke. It jerked along for a few metres while Rachel tried to steer to the side of the narrow dirt road and then, with a final splutter, it died.

Great! Rachel thought grimly. *Another disaster!* Why couldn't things ever just go smoothly? "Why've we stopped?" asked one of the girls.

"Er — car trouble," Rachel muttered. For a few moments everyone sat there, stunned. "Don't worry," she added, sounding more calm than she felt. "Lisa's bound to notice we've stopped. She can go and get help."

Sure enough, a few minutes later Lisa came chugging down the road looking puzzled. "Oh, no!" she exclaimed, as she clambered out of her jeep. "You haven't broken down? What rotten luck!"

"Tell me about it!" retorted Rachel. "Listen, Lisa, I think you'd better get back as fast as you can and get help. There was a garage in that town …" She opened out a local map and pointed.

But Lisa wasn't listening. Instead, she opened up the hood of the jeep and peered at the engine. The girls meanwhile had scrambled down from both jeeps and were idling by the side of the road. Someone suggested opening the ice box, and was about to take out a couple of bottles of drink when

Rachel stopped them.

"Drink, particularly water, is our most precious asset," she warned them. "We don't know how long we're going to be here, and I can't risk letting anyone get dehydrated. I think it would be a good idea to wait for a while."

She was distracted by a squeal from Lisa. "I've got it!" she exclaimed. "It's the oil." She held up a dry dipstick, beaming with triumph.

"That's odd," Rachel frowned. "I know I checked the oil before we left. There were two whole cans."

"Well, at least it's easy to fix," said Lisa. "Hang on, let me just take another look." After a few more minutes of probing and tapping, she looked up again, puzzled. "You're not going to like this," she warned Rachel. "But I think someone's been messing with this engine. You've got an oil leak down there – just a small hole. But it's very neat, just as if it had been made with a drill..."

Rachel paled. "But – but what am I going to do?" she gasped. "I can't drive without oil, can I?"

"Yeah – but you can repair it," said one of the girls, Nadine, who'd sauntered up to watch Lisa's investigation of the engine. "My dad's a mechanic. He showed me a few tricks. What you do is, you just have to bung up the hole temporarily, and then keep checking."

In the end, they decided to use a couple of sticking plasters from the First Aid kit. "Anyone got a pair of tights?" asked Nadine. No one had.

"What on earth would we need tights for?" asked Rachel, beginning to think that Nadine had been sent from heaven.

Nadine grinned. "Oh, just another precaution. I thought we could line the oil tank so the plaster would stick there for longer. No sweat. Pass that bag with the snacks in it."

Lisa and Rachel watched in amazement as Nadine expertly lined the tank with the plastic carrier bag. Then Lisa handed her a couple of cans of oil which she poured in. She waited for a few moments, then looked up with a grin. "Seems to have done the trick," she announced, pleased with herself. "Now we know what the problem is, we'll stop now and again and make sure it's all still working."

Everyone piled back into the jeeps and Rachel cautiously started the engine. After a couple of chugs, it purred into action, and the party was off once again.

About half an hour later they reached a little village – with a petrol station. Nadine tapped Rachel on the shoulder. "I think we should stop for a check," she suggested. So Rachel flashed her lights to warn Lisa, and both jeeps pulled into the garage courtyard.

Nadine checked the oil expertly. "Seems to be holding fine," she pronounced. As she spoke, a shiny BMW drew up next to them with a squeal of tyres and a showering of dust.

"Afternoon, ladies – having a spot of bother, are we?" a familiar voice greeted them. It was Gerald! How did he manage to be in so many places at the same time as she was? Rachel wondered, exasperated.

"Hello, Gerald," she called coolly. Then something odd occurred to her. "What makes you think we're having trouble?" she asked, staring steadily at him.

Gerald flushed. "Oh, nothing, nothing," he assured her. 'Just, you know, bunch of girls gathered round a car engine in the middle of nowhere. Makes you think, dunnit – bound to be something up."

I'll bet that's just what you're thinking! Rachel thought angrily. But she kept her voice as even and calm as she could manage as she commented, "So what brings you out this way?"

Gerald, still flushed, looked confused. "Oh, er ... you know."

"I expect you were on your way to the petrified forest, were you?" Rachel suggested, as if trying to help him out.

He looked relieved, and nodded. "Yeah, something like that..."

"Going to see that mate of yours?" Rachel went on. "Going to check up on him, maybe? Make sure your business deals were in order."

Gerald was speechless for a few moments. Then he managed to mutter, "Better go, ladies, if you're not needing any help. See you later, right?"

"Oh, I think so, yes," Rachel answered. And she felt a surge of satisfaction at the look of dazed confusion on his face.

An hour later they were pulling in to the courtyard of the Hotel Elena. Rachel was quiet and thoughtful, but Lisa was full of beans. She'd enjoyed the adventure and was especially pleased that they'd all got home safely without needing any help.

155

As she switched off the engine and opened the door, she saw Stavros sloping past. "Hey!" she called, so pleased to see him she momentarily forgot that they'd barely spoken for days. "Hey, Stavros! It's me, Lisa!"

Stavros simply walked faster until he'd rounded the corner. Convinced he couldn't have heard her, Lisa went running after him. When she reached the corner she caught a glimpse of his retreating back. He'd nearly reached the door to the reps office when he turned and looked at her.

The smile froze on Lisa's face as he spoke. "Hi, Lisa. Busy right now. Sorry." And he was gone.

Tears sprang to Lisa's eyes as she stumbled back to the jeeps where Rachel was waiting. "He's given me the brush-off," she announced, trying desperately to sound casual. "I'll just have to accept he's not interested, and get back to the way we all were before."

Rachel linked her arm in Lisa's and the two made their way to the apartment at the back of the hotel. As Rachel was unlocking the door, Alex appeared in the corridor. His own room was next door to theirs.

"Hi, you two," he said in a neutral voice. "How did it go? Good trip?" Then Lisa turned to look at him, her face taut with hurt and pent-up emotion.

"Lisa – what's the matter?" he asked, suddenly full of concern.

"Oh, Alex!" she faltered. "We have to talk!" And then she burst into tears.

14

Overcome with concern and tenderness, Alex took Lisa's hand and led her, sobbing, into his room. They sat down on the bed and he took her in his arms. "There, it's OK," he soothed. "If you need to cry, just cry."

But that only made Lisa cry even more piteously. His words, his gentleness as he hugged her and stroked her hair, reminded her sharply of another, very similar occasion. Only last time, when she'd run crying into the arms of a man, it had been Stavros comforting her, after she had encountered Alex and Astrid together.

"Why does everything have to be so difficult?" she managed to gasp eventually, her head still buried in Alex's shoulder. "It used to be so simple."

"We used to be in love," Alex said softly. He tilted Lisa's tear-streaked face to his and kissed her very softly, full on the lips. More than anything, then, she wanted him to kiss away the hurt and pain, to make love to her just as he used to. Perhaps then, she thought wildly, she could forget all about Stavros, and things would be easy again.

But she knew it was impossible. There was no feeling, any more. She pulled her face away and looked into Alex's eyes. All she could read there was a kind of pity.

"It really is over this time, isn't it?" he said quietly.

She nodded. "I wish it wasn't – but it is."

"But we'll always be friends, won't we?" he pressed her anxiously.

Lisa nodded again. "Oh, I hope so, Alex – you're my best friend in the world. You and Rachel. Do you think we can?"

Alex hugged her again. "Of course we can. But on one condition." She looked at him questioningly. "That you tell me what's breaking your heart. Tell me everything – since I'm your very best friend in the world, me and Rachel. And let's see if we can put a plaster on and make it better."

Lisa smiled, happy that at least she and Alex weren't going to be strangers any more. She took a deep breath, and began to talk...

At eight o'clock that same night, in Athens, Jack was sitting at his desk surrounded by piles of paper and running his fingers wildly through his tousled hair. Mariella stood in the doorway watching him.

"It's late, Jack," Mariella said, with a hint of a whine in her voice. "You've done enough tonight. Let's pack it in."

"I can't! You go, but I've got to get through some of this paperwork. Otherwise, I'll drown in it." He banged his fist on the desk in frustration, sending several piles of paper flying into the air.

He and Mariella both dived at the same time to grab the papers. They collided and sprawled to the floor. For a moment, they stared at each other. Then Mariella gave Jack a long, knowing look and stretched out on the floor like a kitten. "How convenient," she murmured. "This is just where I'd hoped to land." She reached out one leg suggestively so that it brushed Jack's thigh.

Dazzled at her nearness, her willingness, the obvious invitation in her voice, Jack lay down beside her. His hand crept round her back and drew her close. Their bodies touched, their lips met, then very slowly Mariella shifted so that she was lying on her back, urging him to cover her whole body with his.

Groaning with desire, Jack allowed her to pull him closer as her hands reached underneath his shirt and her fingers began to dig into his back. "I've been wanting this to happen for so long," she whispered, wrapping her arms round Jack's neck. "And you have, too – haven't you?"

It was as though those words jolted him to his senses. "Mariella – you're lovely," he said hoarsely. "But we can't do this. You know I've got a girlfriend..."

"That doesn't matter," she said, her eyes still closed, her lips full and sensuous. "This is just between us, not anyone else. It was going to happen some time, you know it was. So why not now?"

"Because it would be wrong," Jack answered simply, privately wondering whether he was crazy to give up the chance to make love to this willing, incredibly sexy girl. But he knew he mustn't – not if he valued his relationship with Rachel. Whatever the problems, he was still in love with her and still wanted to make it work. What they had was just too good to throw away.

Wrenching himself from Mariella's arms, Jack hurriedly collected his scattered papers, replaced them on the desk, and headed for the door.

"Where are you going?" Mariella asked forlornly, still on the floor.

"Out," he said shortly. "There's somewhere I have to go."

"But I thought you were staying on here," she protested petulantly. "You said you had to work. Let's work together and then—"

"No!" Jack rasped. "Can't you see, that's not going to happen. I guess I should really be working, but I've got to do something more urgent."

As he closed the door behind him he heard muffled sobs and felt a momentary regret. What harm would it have done, to have stayed there with Mariella? Why had he walked out on her?

But he knew the reason all too well. Rachel. That encounter with Mariella had confirmed how he felt about Rachel. And it had made him realize what he had to do. He had to see Rachel now. Urgently. He had to clear up all the confusion and suspicion so that they could be together again. In love. Just like they used to be.

*   *   *

While Jack was waiting for the evening boat which would take him to Ephros in under two hours, Rachel sat at her favourite table in Andy's Taverna – right on the edge of the beach. She was sipping a thick, sweet brew of coffee and trying to compose her thoughts so that she would be calm and in control when Gerald finally appeared.

As soon as she and Lisa had returned from their dramatic adventures, she'd written a curt note to Gerald asking him to meet her tonight. It was high time she discovered the truth, she told herself grimly.

It wasn't long before his cheerful figure ambled into sight. He greeted her with a friendly wave, clearly untroubled by their earlier confrontation, or by the cold, set expression on her face. "Hello, doll," he began easily as he reached the table and sat down. "Got a prob, then? You don't look all that chipper, I must say. Why don't you tell your Uncle Gerry all about it?"

Rachel remained silent and furious while he ordered his coffee and a bottle of wine. How could he pretend there was nothing wrong? And how could she have been taken in by him?

"Gerald, my jeep was deliberately tampered with today," she said. "A hole was drilled in the oil tank."

"Oh, that's too bad," Gerald said, his voice laden with sympathy.

"Come off it," she went on, her eyes glinting. "I'm not that stupid. You got your friend at the petrified forest to do it, didn't you?"

There was a pause. Gerald seemed to be

weighing up his thoughts. Then he grinned. "It's a fair cop," he admitted. "But it's all for your own good, darlin'."

"I just don't believe this!" Rachel flared. "First of all you admit to – a criminal act that could have caused a really serious accident. Or we could have been stranded in the desert and died of dehydration. Or murdered. And you tell me it's for my own good."

"Don't get so rattled," Gerald said irritatingly. "It is for your own good. See, I've been doing a lot of business on your behalf. If you play your cards right, you could do very well out of my little dealings this summer."

Rachel stared at him open-mouthed. The vague suspicions that had been cluttering her mind, like pieces of a jigsaw puzzle, began to merge into a blurred but sinister picture. "This isn't the only disaster you've caused, is it?" she said slowly. "That time they wouldn't let our boat land after the trip to Turkey – I had a hunch you had something to do with that. You did, didn't you?"

"That's right," Gerald agreed affably. "I drink in that bar all the time, got chatting with a few mates. It was no problem fixing that little panic with the harbour officials and then engaging the good doctor in a few – erm – jars of medicine."

Rachel was beginning to feel as though she was in the grip of a strange nightmare. "And the little girl who went missing," she went on faintly. "Who just happened to show up on the beach where I was – just after I'd had a drink with you."

"She wasn't going to come to any harm," said

Gerald. "It wasn't for long, anyhow. And like I say, it's all in a good cause, isn't it?"

"What are you talking about?" Rachel shouted at him. "You must be crazy! I don't understand why you want to cause all this damage – but it certainly isn't being done for me! How could it be?"

"Ah, well, depends how you look at it," Gerald said, refusing to be rattled. "Remember the night I introduced you to Socrates Kolynos? He's one of the most influential businessmen round these islands. And he, er – he wants to get a foothold in the package holiday business. He's very interested in Dream Ticket, you know. It's got a lot going for it, but it's too small to operate the way it should. Your local suppliers, the hotels and apartment owners – he reckons they deserve something a bit better."

Rachel remembered all the conversations with the Ilyaki family – all Gerald's chance remarks about how they could make so much more money if they expanded. She recalled all his criticisms of Dream Ticket – his suggestions for how they could charge more, offer more, own more.

"So – so you've been trying to make us look inefficient, so that all the local businesses will stop trusting us," she said slowly, barely able to believe her own words. "You've just been preparing the way for a nasty, hostile take-over?"

Gerald nodded happily. "Don't look so shocked, darlin'," he told her. "It'll be great for you. Why do you think I wanted you to meet my old mate Socrates? I knew you'd impress him, see? I've been telling him what a great girl you are. How you're much too good for that tinpot little outfit you work for. I'm doin' you a favour, Rachel. You'll get far more money, far more prospects, everything…"

"Don't I get a say in this?" asked Rachel. "Or didn't that cross your mind when you were making all your plans? As it happens, Dream Ticket works well just because it is so small. We can give better customer care, that way. We respect local communities and don't try to develop them so much that all their character is lost. I think that's a much better way to approach tourism."

"Well, you may think that," retorted Gerald. "But that's just some sentimental idea of preserving little pockets of unspoilt Europe for your English tourists. That's who you're thinking about, isn't it? Not the local businesses. Believe me, if you offer them a choice between preserving a bit of culture or earning a lot more dough I think I know what they'd choose. And nice Mr Kolynos, who incidentally comes from this very island himself, knows the people far better than you do."

Rachel was so angry she couldn't speak for a while. Unflustered, Gerald drained his glass of retsina, then filled Rachel's glass and his own. "So, how about it, then?"

"How about what?" Rachel asked coldly.

"I'm offering you a job – right now," Gerald said. "Obviously there's a lot of negotiations still to do and the deal hasn't actually gone through. But I'm not the hanging-around type. I like to get things sorted. So – come and work for me and my business now, then when Dream Ticket is formally sold to the Socrates empire you will be taken on as one of their executive managers. How does that sound?"

"It sounds like rubbish," spat Rachel. "I wouldn't touch it, or you, if it were the last job offer on earth."

She got up to leave, but Gerald was too quick for her. He, too, rose from his seat and blocked her way. "Think about what I'm offering – the prospects are pretty irresistible."

"Not to me, they're not," blazed Rachel. "And what's even worse, I feel so stupid! I trusted you, Gerald. I liked you. We had such good times together. And now you've betrayed me."

Her voice cracked and, to her fury, her eyes filled with tears. Gerald held his face very close to hers, viewing her distress with satisfaction. "You'll come round to my way of thinking, doll," he told her confidently. "And besides – I always fancied you, you know." He planted a rather wet kiss on her mouth.

There was a resounding crack as Rachel slapped his face. "Well, I never fancied you!" she flung back. "And just leave me alone from now on, Gerald, because I will never, repeat never, change my mind. Read my lips. Never."

As Gerald slouched away, deflated, another figure crouched quietly watching, just a few metres away. Jack had been there for quite some time. Hidden by bushes, he'd managed to catch some but not all of the conversation. But he was left in very little doubt about what he'd witnessed.

Rachel and the man from the snapshot had been sitting close together, drinking wine and talking intently. They had grappled for a few moments, but it was clear that was just a lovers' tiff. He could hear a few telling words wafting in the breeze. *"I trusted you, Gerald. I liked you. We had such good times together. And now you've betrayed me."* And, as if to confirm his suspicions, the man had actually kissed her.

Almost blinded with rage and grief Jack stumbled out of the bushes with a crash. Rachel looked up, startled. "Jack!" she yelled.

"Yes, Jack!" he snarled. "Surprised, are you? I don't suppose you expected me, did you? You did seem rather busy." He strode towards her, his face a mask of hurt anger.

"How could you, Rachel?" he demanded in disgust.

"How could I what?" Rachel asked in a strangled voice. Then, with dawning despair, she began to understand what Jack must be thinking. "Oh, no – no! Jack, listen, it's not what you think."

"Oh, really?" Jack commented with ugly sarcasm. "I suppose you're going to tell me you've never met the man who happened to be kissing you."

"Of course not," Rachel answered, confused. "I mean, of course I do, I know him – but that's all. That was the only time he's ever kissed me, and I was trying to stop him. None of this is how it seems. There's nothing between us, nothing!"

"Come off it, Rachel – you must think I'm really

stupid. What do you think this is then, eh?" Jack scrabbled in his pocket, pulled out the crumpled photograph of Rachel with Gerald and brandished it in front of her face.

Rachel gaped at the photo in horror. It was like being confronted by a nightmare. "Where did that come from?" she asked in a faint whisper.

"Does it really matter?" Jack asked wearily, as though his worst fears had been confirmed. "All that matters is that you are a lying, scheming two-timer who's deceived me and deceived Dream Ticket."

"I haven't! It's not true!" protested Rachel urgently. "Jack, you've got to believe me. I love you. *I love you!*"

But Jack wasn't listening. He'd turned his back and was walking bitterly away.

He decided to go to bed — they'd find him a spare room in the Elena. Tomorrow, he'd have to confront Rachel. Right now, all he wanted to do was sleep. And cry.

15

The next morning after breakfast Rachel called an emergency meeting of the reps on her balcony. She'd had a wretched, sleepless night, fretting about Jack, longing to see him and trying to work out what she would say to make him believe her. But when she'd gone to look for him in the morning he'd already left, leaving her feeling more wretched than ever. Now, though, she was forcing herself to concentrate on the problems facing Dream Ticket.

Bleary-eyed, she glanced round at the unhappy little gathering. Lisa looked tearful and strained – Alex worried and protective. Stavros, who had arrived late, was even more silent than usual and refused to meet Lisa's eye. Only Alison looked calm and happy – almost smug, thought Rachel. Obviously she was deliriously in love.

As soon as Rachel began to tell the others about her conversation with Gerald, about the times he had deliberately caused problems for them, the work he was doing to help Socrates take over Dream Ticket, their personal quarrels were forgotten. Everyone sat up and listened, open-eyed.

"Ugh — I can't believe you let him kiss you," shuddered Lisa. "I mean — he's so yuk!"

"The whole thing's yuk," added Alex, his brow wrinkled in a frown of distress and concentration. "It's a nasty tale, Rachel, but it doesn't quite make sense, somehow. I mean, if Kolynos is so well-known round here, why would he bother to discredit us like this? He wouldn't need to convince the people that he would be better to deal with."

Rachel nodded. "I was wondering about that, too," she agreed. "And what's more, I don't think it's been working, has it? The Ilyakis like Gerald. They've probably been a bit tempted by all his talk about expansion and profitability and all that stuff. But they like us, too. I don't think anything that's happened has put them off us."

"That's partly because we've managed to head off most of the problems, though," Lisa put in. "Things could have been far worse. That day at the hot springs, remember, Alison? Now that could have been a real disaster, but we just dealt with it fast and people had quite a good time in the end."

Rachel looked puzzled. "Gerald didn't mention that one — but you're probably right. He could easily have fixed up that little disaster. He'd recommended the hot springs, hadn't he?"

Lisa nodded. "He knew the bloke — just like he

always knows everyone. The manager was expecting us. I thought it was peculiar at the time, didn't you, Alison?"

Alison nodded thoughtfully. "But what I don't get is – why would that put off the accommodation owners? It's not their problem if an outing goes wrong."

"Suppose it's just all part of making us look inefficient," said Rachel. "But I agree, it doesn't quite make sense. Hang on, let's think. Have there been any other little incidents that could have been caused by him?"

Alex leaned back, his eyes closed. "This summer has been one long string of disasters," he said. "How can we possibly single out any of them? That day we ran out of water, for instance. That could have hit the Ilyakis pretty hard."

"Exactly!" said Rachel excitedly. "And I'll bet it was Gerald who caused it, too. Remember how he's always on at them to install more efficient plumbing!"

"There was one other," said Stavros slowly. "The other night, when our boat was late." For the first time for several days he looked over at Lisa and caught her eye. She blushed. Both of them were remembering, with a shock, that magical day together, ending in that electrifying kiss in the moonlight as the boat finally tugged into the harbour. It was almost as if an invisible cord bound them together as they stared at each other, locked into the same memory.

"Oh, no," said Alison vehemently. They all turned to her, surprised.

"I can't believe that!" she went on. "In fact, I know that can't be right. The local trips are the part of the business that Tony runs. He would never dream of trying to sabotage Dream Ticket. In fact, he was really cross over that mix-up. He hates it when things don't run smoothly. He gave his crew a really hard time, but it wasn't their fault. Someone had called to alter the booking. They still haven't found out who."

"I can guess, though," said Rachel grimly. "Maybe Gerald's story wasn't quite accurate. Maybe he wasn't working for Kolynos all this time after all."

"He can't have been!" Alison was shaking her head passionately. "I know Tony wouldn't have anything to do with dirty dealings, and from what he tells me, his dad wouldn't either. In fact, I'm sure he said his dad thinks Gerald's a bit of a joke."

"That wouldn't stop him using him, if he needed him," put in Alex. "You can get someone to do your dirty work without being their best friend."

"Can you find out more, Alison?" Rachel asked. "If you're right, it must mean that Gerald's up to something else."

"Well, maybe he's in it for himself," suggested Lisa. "Maybe it isn't Socrates Kolynos who wants to buy out Dream Ticket at all, but Gerald himself."

"OK, I'll see what I can find out," promised Alison. "Tony's coming to the disco tonight – at the Elena."

"Oh, no – I'd forgotten about that!" groaned

Alex. "All those teenagers spilling shandy and shrieking and getting into fights. Remember the Hot Club?"

"How could we forget?" said Lisa and Rachel together. They all laughed.

"Right," said Rachel in a more businesslike voice. "What are we up to today? Alex – a football session with the boys this morning, then office duty this afternoon, yes? Alison and Stavros – hotel and apartment routine visits. Lisa – did you say you were doing a women's aqua-splash today? Right, I'll do the Seashell Club – there are only four of them booked in today. We'll meet up at the disco, shall we?"

As everyone dispersed Stavros was still staring darkly at Lisa. "Could I – have a word with you?" he stammered. He followed her out of Rachel's room and into her own.

"Lisa – I'm sorry," he said, taking her hand. "I have been behaving badly. You see, that day in Tykonos, and then that kiss..."

Lisa raised her eyes to his, as a little ray of hope lit her heart.

"I haven't been able to think straight since then," Stavros told her. "One minute, I think it means nothing. Then I remember – and I know I want you so much. Then I think you are still with Alex. Then I am not so sure. And me – I am bad news. It is not good to get involved with me, I think."

"Oh, Stavros!" Lisa sighed. "That is just so vain of you. Why do men always boast the whole time?"

"No – this was not a boast," protested Stavros.

"It is true. I am afraid of getting close to you. I am afraid of hurting you."

"Well, that's daft," Lisa told him firmly. "What makes you think I'm going to get hurt, in any case?"

Stavros suddenly felt very happy, very sure of what had to happen. He pulled Lisa towards him and kissed her softly. "All I know is that this feels right," he whispered.

"Yes," agreed Lisa. "Let's not make things complicated, when really they can be so very simple." And then they kissed again.

Jack, too, had been awake for most of the night, torn between fury at Rachel and despair at losing her. He'd just fallen into an exhausted, troubled sleep when he was awoken by the shrill of the telephone, and the loud, affable voice of his boss, Theo. "There you are!" he boomed down the line. "I'm in Athens, on business. Are you coming back? There's a lot we have to talk over."

So Jack had scrambled into his clothes and rushed off to catch the boat. He'd just have to come back tonight, he resolved. He'd break it off there and then and finally Rachel would be out of his system once and for all.

Theo was waiting for him when he arrived at the office, dishevelled and breathless, a couple of hours later. 'Jack! Good to see you! Glad to see you're getting out into the field checking up on the resorts. That's what the travel business is all about, after all. It's sun, sea, food and romance — not purchase orders and insurance forms in triplicate. Too many managers these days spend all their time sitting hunched at a desk, paper-pushing."

"Well I've been guilty of that over the last few weeks," admitted Jack. "I've never had so many errors – which means I've spent far too much time trying to trace them and sort them out. Some accounts haven't been fully paid, some of our bookings have been inaccurate. I just can't get the books to balance."

"That's one of the reasons I'm here," Theo announced. "I was aware that for some time there have been irregularities here. Now I know you're a reliable manager, Jack. There had to be some other reason. So I've been doing a bit of digging, and I've discovered what's been going on. You're being set up, lad."

Jack ran his fingers distractedly through his hair, as he always did when harassed. What was Theo trying to tell him now? Wasn't it enough that his private life was on the rocks? Now it sounded as though his job was rocketing into major trauma.

"I had a trace put on some of the bookings that have been causing you problems and followed that up with a bit more investigation. Those bookings were all traceable to one business – holding several accounts, in different banks in different cities, but one business nevertheless. Something called Fantasy Holdings. Each bank account was in a different name, but they were all directors of the same company. If, that is, they exist at all. It seems more likely they're all the same person, the Managing Director and Chief Executive of Fantasy. Fellow by the name of Gerald Birt. Name mean anything?"

Jack shook his head. He was so stunned by Theo's announcement that he couldn't say anything for a while. Theo cast him a searching look, then handed him a tattered photograph. It was identical to the one that had been sent anonymously to him – Rachel, laughing, right up close to a slightly overweight, balding, middle-aged man.

"That's the one I mean," Theo said. "Thought you might have come across him, since that's one of your reps he's with. Seems he's been hanging around Ephros all summer, making trouble."

"But – but why?" Jack stammered out eventually.

"Well, I'll admit I didn't work this out all by myself," Theo told him. "My old mate Socrates Kolynos has been a great help. Seems this Gerald Birt has been smarming up to him for months, trying to interest him in some sort of investment in his Fantasy Company. Socrates wasn't interested, but he did agree to find out whether it was likely that Dream Ticket was up for grabs."

"That's right," Jack remembered. "He came to see me. I couldn't understand what he wanted, told him to get in touch with you."

"That's right," nodded Theo. "He did. He got in touch to warn me that Gerald was after my company, and probably after my staff. That girl I mentioned to you, Rachel Stanley." He tapped the photograph, and Jack looked away. "Seems I wasn't the only one to have spotted her talent. Gerald Birt was keen to lure her away from us. Very keen, as a matter of fact. According to my mate Socrates she wasn't playing ball. His son's in with that crowd, apparently, so he brings home one version, Gerald gives him another."

Jack was still too stunned to say much. Was it possible? he wondered. Could it be that Rachel had been set up? If that photograph had been copied and sent to two major Dream Ticket executives, it certainly looked likely.

"So — this trouble you've been having here, it's all part of Birt's tactics to undermine the good name and efficiency of Dream Ticket. Just to make it easier for him to move in. And he's been causing no end of trouble for your reps out there, too."

Jack remembered Rachel's worried phone calls, when she'd tell him of the disasters of her day. She certainly hadn't linked them together. Neither had he. But now, suddenly, all those details were beginning to fall into place.

"So anyhow," Theo went on, "now we know, we can act. I think I've probably got enough on our friend Mr Birt to see that he won't be causing us any more grief. And by the way, it's time we did something about young Rachel. Remember, I mentioned before that I thought we should be offering her something in the Marbella office. What do you reckon?"

"Fine, good idea," mumbled Jack. He probably would have said the same thing if Theo had suggested sending Rachel to manage the Dream Ticket satellite office on the moon. Because all that mattered right now was getting back to Ephros, back to Rachel, and finding out once and for all whether there was any chance of salvaging their love affair.

It was almost dark. The Hotel Elena's dining patio had been cleared to make a dance floor, with tables dotted round the edges. A barbecue was sizzling invitingly, and a string of fairy lights had been laced through the olive and date trees.

"It is pretty, yes?" Maggi Ilyaki commented to Rachel.

"Gorgeous," agreed Rachel. "You are wonderful, making all this effort."

Maggi shrugged. "I like to do it. Of course it is hard work – for all of us. My daughter Thea, she has been working all day in the kitchen; Michael, he is at the bar. Everyone has to help out. But they are good children and we all like to make the visitors happy. It is good to see them enjoy themselves."

"You could probably fill the place with teenagers all summer if you wanted to," said Rachel, remembering the popularity of the Hot Club.

"Oh, no." Maggi shook her head. "I would not like to do that. You know, your friend Gerald, he tries to persuade us to build, build, get bigger and bigger. At first I say to my husband, Michael, we should really think about these things. Maybe we could be rich, yes? But Michael, he thinks it's better to be happy, and to do things the way we do them. And maybe he is right. It would not be good to get too big. We would lose our own ways..."

Rachel smiled warmly at her. Maggi was confirming what she had suspected. That people are not all as greedy and ambitious as Gerald thought – nothing like as greedy as he was, in fact. And it was reassuring that after all their mishaps, the Ilyakis still wanted to please Dream Ticket and its clients.

Soon the tables were crowded with excited young people, the DJ had put on some loud Greek music as an ice breaker, and the party had begun. Some people jostled at the trestle table groaning with salads and grilled meat. Others had already taken to the floor.

Rachel noticed Stavros and Lisa, dancing very close, even though the music was lively and up tempo. Even closer, swaying together cheek to cheek, were Alison and Tony. Alex was dancing with four young girls at once, while another four seemed to be scrabbling to get near him. All of them were in high spirits and shrieking with laughter. Rachel smiled wistfully as she surveyed the scene. Maybe, she told herself, just maybe things were getting back to normal – at least for everyone else.

Then there wasn't time to wonder about anything else, because someone was screaming: "Fire!" And sure enough, a blaze had broken out in one of the trees, and was spreading fast. Everyone was suddenly shrieking in panic and moving in all directions.

Rachel fought through the crowds to where the DJ stood on stage and grabbed his microphone. "OK, everyone, calm down. Calm down. I want you out of here in single files, otherwise someone will get hurt. Everyone over that side of the table, follow Alex over there. Everyone here, where Lisa is – follow her. Now – no pushing, just move, so we can deal with this fire. And calm down."

As she did her best to soothe the crowd and direct them safely away from the dance floor, Stavros and Alex, with Michael and Maggi and their son Michael, were chucking buckets of water over the fast-spreading flames. Michael was shouting for someone to fetch the extinguishers, but he couldn't bear to leave the fire himself.

"I hope the fire engine will be here soon," he panted. "But you know, they are not always prompt. It is a small service..."

The rest of his words were obliterated as, with a deafening crash, the wooden fencing round the dance floor collapsed. At the same time, all the supports that held the roof over the dining patio came roaring down.

Desperately, Michael and his son turned the extinguishers on the raging blaze, but it was too powerful. "Water!" Michael yelled. "We must have more water!" But he was shouting in vain. The plumbing of the Hotel Elena, unused to coping with such a demand, had collapsed once again. Nothing was coming out of the taps.

Rachel headed over the garden to the swimming pool. She remembered the hose that Michael always used to fill it when it had been cleaned. Provided this water supply was still working, that powerful jet could surely be harnessed against the fast-spreading blaze?

Soon she was tugging urgently at the hose, pulling it out of the box behind the bar, desperately trying to hook it to a tap. But her hands were trembling so hard she could barely control them. She was sobbing with terror and frustration when she heard a reassuring, calm voice beside her.

"Great idea," Jack told her. "Just hook it here and let's pray there's still a supply." Swiftly, he hooked up the hose, put the tap on full and passed the other end to Michael's son, who rushed with it towards the blaze. But even that was not enough to stem the spreading flames.

"Water! We must have more water!" everyone was screaming at once.

"Bring the buckets here!" shrieked Rachel. "There's plenty of water!" And somehow she and Jack managed to organize everyone into a line from the pool right back to where the blaze was taking an even firmer hold.

Just as it seemed they were beginning to get the worst of the fire under control there was a scream from Alison, near the front of the bucket-line. She was pointing to the kitchen. Poisonous smoke and vicious flames were bursting out through the door.

"Oh, no! The fire must have swept in from the barbecue!" shouted Stavros.

"But Thea is in there!" wailed Maggi, with a piercing shriek. "Thea — was in there." Almost hysterical, she tried to rush into the blazing kitchen but Jack restrained her. All round them, increasingly hysterical groups were rushing in all directions, some anxious to help with the fire, others in sheer panic.

In the middle of the chaos, Rachel noticed a lifeless figure, lying in the bushes. "Thea's here!" she shouted to Maggi. "It's OK – she must have got out!"

Rachel rushed over to the girl's limp body. She had obviously been overcome with fumes before staggering out and collapsing. She wasn't breathing. Hurriedly, Rachel turned the girl on to her back, swept ash and the remains of charred hair from her face, and ran her finger lightly into her throat to make sure there were no blockages. Then, steadily and confidently, she held the girl's mouth open and began to give her the kiss of life.

It seemed ages before Thea's body reacted. Then, suddenly, she jerked to life and began to choke.

Then, at last, the fire brigade arrived and, amid a lot of rushing and shouting, managed at last to control the blaze. Maggi was clasping her daughter tightly and crying. Michael had produced a bottle of strong Greek brandy and insisted that they all sit down and drink.

"To my emergency service," Jack whispered to Rachel, gently clinking her glass.

She looked up at him in wonder. It had seemed so natural to have Jack by her side in the emergency – so often before they had worked together like this in the face of disaster. It was only now that the crisis had passed that she remembered that just the previous evening, the last time she'd seen him, she'd honestly wondered if they'd ever meet again.

"Jack — what are you doing here?" she asked. "I — I thought—"

"Don't say it," Jack said quickly. "I love you. I've always loved you. And if you love me too, that's all that matters, all that ever could matter."

And then she was in his arms, tears of emotion and joy filling her eyes as he held her close.

The next afternoon Rachel lay dozing by the pool, surrounded by grapes and figs, apricots and delicious honey-coated home-made pastries. They were all gifts from a grateful Maggi, for saving her daughter's life.

"The Ilyakis are so generous," she remarked to Jack, who lounged beside her. "Here they are with a burnt-out kitchen and a ruined patio at the height of the holiday season, and instead of blaming us, they're showering us with gifts."

"Well, maybe they value their daughter's life more than their property," suggested Jack tenderly. "I was awfully proud of you, you know. And besides, the Ilyakis know now that the fire was started deliberately."

"We should have guessed, shouldn't we?" Rachel said. "He seemed like such an easy-going, friendly bloke, Gerald. But he hated not getting his own way. It must have been his one last act of spite."

"The irony is, he'd already been arrested," Jack told her. "Theo had got on to the cops and they picked him up at the airport. I suppose he'd decided to disappear for a while, so they wouldn't connect him with the fire. But Rachel, what I don't understand is that if there really was nothing between you, why didn't you ever mention him?"

Rachel shrugged. "I suppose there were always better things to talk about. And then, after a while, it seemed a bit awkward to bring his name up when I'd known him for weeks and you'd never heard of him. I guess I was afraid you might get the wrong idea about him."

"I got the wrong idea because you didn't mention him," Jack pointed out. "Still, I should have realized from that picture he wasn't your type."

He leaned over and kissed her – a long, lazy kiss. A kiss that said they were together again, happier and more in love than ever.

Rachel sighed, sinking into the wonderful, warm feeling of being with the man she loved and knowing that they belonged together.

Jack hadn't told her yet about Theo's idea of sending her to Marbella. It was too far off to worry about. Maybe he'd go to Spain himself. Maybe he'd be sent somewhere completely different. It didn't matter. However far apart they were, they'd always belong together in their hearts.

The following Saturday, Alex and Lisa were waiting at the airport for the next batch of Dream Ticket holiday-makers – Lisa bouncy and excited, Alex quiet and wistful. He was quite resigned now to seeing Lisa and Stavros together. It had stopped hurting. Now, as the new crowd began to appear through the door of the little baggage area, he began to feel positively glad things had worked out as they had.

A group of three girls of about his own age appeared, all very pretty, all chattering excitedly. Alex thought they all looked nice, really. He felt a terrific sense of freedom.

"Hey, are you the Dream Ticket rep?" asked one of the girls.

"Wow, the holiday's started to look good already!" said another, admiringly.

"Which way's the coach?" they clamoured. "Where's the resort?"

Alex smiled at them and pointed. "Just follow the sun," he said.

Someone squeezed his arm. It was Lisa, her eyes twinkling mischievously. "That's what you should do," she whispered. "Follow the sun! I mean, I think the blonde one fancies you and I absolutely know that one in the middle in the tiny shorts does. If I were you, I'd just go where it looks hottest!"

As she spoke, Alex was filled with a sense of hope and elation. The summer stretched before him, week after week of new people, new faces, new possibilities. It was like starting a new adventure – the dawn of a new day.

P●INT CRiME

If you like Point Horror, you'll love Point Crime!
A murder has been committed ...Whodunnit? Was it
the arch rival, the mystery stranger or the best friend?
An exciting series of crime novels, with tortuous plots
and lots of suspects, designed to keep the reader
guessing till the very last page.

POINT FANTASY

Read Point Fantasy and escape into the realms of the imagination; the kingdoms of mortal and immortal elements. Lose yourself in the world of the dragon and the dark lord, the princess and the mage; a world where magic rules and the forces of evil are ever poised to attack…

Doom Sword
Peter Beere
Adam discovers the Doom Sword and has to face a perilous quest…

Brog the Stoop
Joe Boyle
Can Brog restore the Source of Light to Drabwurld?

Book of Shadows
Stan Nicholls
Magic so terrible as to be beyond imagining…

The Renegades Series:
Book 1: Healer's Quest
Book 2: Fire Wars
Book 3: The Return of the Wizard
Jessica Palmer
Journey with Zelia and Ares as they combine their magical powers to battle against evil and restore order to their land…

Realms of the Gods
Tamora Pierce
The barrier's gone … and no one's in control…